BLOOD ROYAL

"Had the king lived, there had been no murder of womenfolk; but Bedfort had shot down the king from behind and fled to Mackinac, untouched of the law, and the kingdom had fallen into hands weaker and more cruel. Therefore had come voyageur, lumberjack, fisherman, bearing with them retribution." Here in two sentences is the setting of this, the latest of H. Bedford-Jones' remarkable romances, which is also his best. The proof of the story is in the reading.

WILDSIDE PULP CLASSICS

The Blind Spot, by Austin Hall and Homer Eon Flint
Amazon Nights, by Arthur O. Friel
Far Below & Other Horrors, edited by Robert Weinberg
The Golden Dolphin, by J. Allan Dunn
The Grand Cham, by Harold Lamb
Murgunstruum and Others, by Hugh B. Cave
The Opium Ship, by H. Bedford Jones
Out of the Wreck, by Captain A.E. Dingle
The Slayer and Other Tales, by H. de Vere Stacpoole
Wings over Tomorrow, by Philip F. Nowlan

BY JOHNSTON MCCULLEY

Black Star
The Mark of Zorro
The Spider Strain and Other Tales from the Pulps
Tales of Thubway Tham

BY ROBERT E. HOWARD

The Complete Action Stories
Gates of Empire
Graveyard Rats
Moon of Skulls
Shadow Kingdoms
Treasures of Tartary
Waterfront Fists

BY CLARK ASHTON SMITH

The Double Shadow
The Maker of Gargoyles

PULP MAGAZINE FACSIMILES

The Black Mask Magazine, No. 2 (May 1920)
Ghost Stories (June 1931)
The Phantom Detective #1 (February 1933)
Sinister Stories (February 1940)
Spicy Mystery Stories (August 1935)
Spicy Mystery Stories (February 1937)
Strange Tales #7 (January 1933)
Submarine Stories (March 1930)
Tales of Magic and Mystery (February 1928)
The Thrill Book, (Sept. 1, 1919)
Weird Trails, (April 1933)

THE MYSTERIOUS WU FANG

The Case of the Suicide Tomb, by Robert J. Hogan

OPERATOR #5

The Army of the Dead, by Curtis Steele
Blood Reign of the Dictator, by Curtis Steele
Invasion of the Crimson Death Cult, by Curtis Steele
Liberty's Suicide Legions, by Curtis Steele
Revolt of the Devil Men, by Curtis Steele
Winged Hordes of the Yellow Vulture, by Curtis Steele

SECRET AGENT "X"

Legion of the Living Dead, by Brant House
Claws of the Corpse Cult, by Brant House

BLOOD ROYAL

H. Bedford-Jones

WILDSIDE PRESS

Published by
Wildside Press, LLC
www.wildsidepress.com

Blood Royal originally appeared
in the December, 1914 issue
of *The People's Magazine.*

CHAPTER I
THE DAY OF RAIDING

Alec Brosseau did not like it, could not reconcile himself to the thing. Yet to him, as to the others, it was a stern, terrible duty which would brook neither delay nor compromise. It is not the way of the North to compromise in her retributions; and since that canoe had drifted to Arbre Croche bearing the slain Bennet with his murdered wife and child, a flame of vengeance had swept through the north woods.

Had the king lived, there had been no murder of womenfolk; but Bedfort had shot down the king from behind and fled to Mackinac, untouched of the law, and the kingdom had fallen into hands weaker and more cruel. Therefore had come voyageur, lumberjack, fisherman, bearing with them retribution. It was this thought which Brosseau voiced as he leaned on his long rifle and faced young McCurdy with undisguised dislike.

"Ver' bad business, ver' bad! But dese people, he's be go too far, bah goss! De king she's be de smugglair, de wreckair, mebbe, but de king's be dead now. All de same, M'sso McCurdy, you be sorry for dis one day. Ah'm be sorry mahself, mebbe."

He paused, a little flame of anger glinting in his dark eyes.

"If we do not'ing, dem Mormon get worse, eh? Ah'm not say for do not'ing, non, non! But to scattair, to scattair de husban' from de wife, de modair from de chil', Ah'm tell you she's be de bad business, McCurdy. You dam Irish!"

Young McCurdy looked down at Cap Wagley's schooner lying in the bay, and turned away with a hard laugh. He had loot to think of. But Brosseau still leaned on his long rifle and watched, his bronzed features stern and sad. After all, he reflected, retribution was far overdue.

Below, near the schooner *Able* which had brought the raiders from the mainland, the ancient steamer *Wisconsin* lay lined at the end of the long wharf, her red side paddles ominous in the sunlight. Over her, and over all the harbor, hovered a low sound of wailing as of many hushed voices.

Out along the lengthy dock, between the piles of cut fuel wood, wended the last of that mournful procession — the last of those who had not fled before the raiders by canoe or fishing boat. The women wept; the men marched, stern and proud, expecting that miracle which came not; the children wondered and wailed; and driving them on were the slim, lithe woodsmen with rifles who had come from the mainland. Here and there flitted one or two deeper-chested, more brutal men, birds of ill omen; already McCurdy foresaw the day when he and his people were to drive forth the voyageur from lakes and timber camp. And Alec Brosseau saw it also, but more dimly.

Another little group came on — the last of all — past the dwellings they had hewed from the wilderness, leaving behind them the wealth they had garnered in devious ways. Their kingdom had reached its end appointed. As they passed the gutted, smoking ruins of their tabernacle, low wails broke from some; but for the most part they moved on in stern martyrdom, past the yellow-belching ashes of the printery, past the sacked log palace of the king, down to the wharf where the red paddle wheels shone like bloody teeth in the afternoon sun.

So had they come, by ones and twos, as they were fetched from the woods and the farther settlements — those of them who had not fled. Up from Lake Galilee, up by the king's highway to the sand crests of Mount Pisgah, up from Gennesaret to the town of Saint James on the bay where the evil-omened steamer awaited them. For long years there had been battle and blood between fisherman, lumberjack, and Mormon; from the Beavers all the coast had been dominated by the king. Now that the king was dead, the raiders were making an utter end of his people.

Watching motionless from the hill, Brosseau's face went grim. He knew what these poor folk did not — that they were going forth to a terrible ending. Man from woman, child from mother, all were to be borne out and scattered, one from the other, along all the shores of Lake Michigan. For retribution had come, engulfing innocent and guilty alike.

In that moment the soul of Alec Brosseau — the tender, visionary French-Canadian soul mingled with the sterner mysticism of his Indian blood — was uppermost. Judgment had come upon these Mormons, because they had sinned, but he knew that it was too harsh a judgment. There had been wrecking, smuggling, treason, defiance of law and government; there had been a kingdom established in the northland, and the northland was spewing it forth in wreck and ruin. But Alec Brosseau remembered the wondrous voice, the great mind, the black heart of the dead King Strang, and his own heart was sore within him.

What was to come afterward? Alec had been mail runner, fisherman, trapper, everything, and he knew the northern shores and their people as few men did. His soul boded ill as he saw the powerful figure of young McCurdy swagger away; it was this Irishman who had taken command of all, and Brosseau shook his head sadly. He saw another kingdom set up where Strang's had been; a more lawless, more powerful, more unscrupulous king at its head. He thought of the lumber camps where the deeper-chested men were already sifting through, and as a burst of wailing drifted up from the bay he sighed and strode away. His heart was tender for these people, despite their sins in the eyes of the north woods.

He looked out across the level sands, and beyond the lighthouse, where the dead lay unmarked the whole length of the Beavers — Mormon dead and French dead, where that secret strife had flamed over fish net and woman, over siscowet and squaw. Now that the end had come, who was profiting by this raid? Not his own people, thought Alec bitterly; only Cap Wagley, of the schooner *Able*, and his younger friend, McCurdy.

So, in the end, it was accomplished. The evening had fallen, the last log farmhouse had given up its living, the steamer had weighed anchor and vanished for the last time. Brosseau, with no heart in him for reveling, sat by the scarred whipping post, and heard the shouts of the feasters come from the castle King Strang had built. To him it was a terrible thing. Some one must pay for it all in the end.

A dark shape broke from the shadows and came slowly toward him, its golden hair flying in the moonglow. Alec's hand fell to his rifle, then he paused to stare into a wide, childish face, into clear gray eyes. The shape was a boy, scarce able to walk, no doubt left behind by his own people. Brosseau, who had thought it a ghost, relaxed.

"Bah goss!" he cried. "What are —"

"I want to go home!" said the boy calmly, quite self-possessed. "You take me."

Alec stared at him, startled of a sudden. That high brow, golden hair, gray-green eyes — even the calm authority in the boyish voice! Could it be possible? "What you' name?" he asked quickly.

But this the boy could not tell him.

"Take me home, daddy," he cried, and put his head down on Alec's knee, wearied, and his clear treble drifted off into sleepy accents. "Take — me home — daddy!"

Brosseau looked down, then glanced around, half alarmed lest anyone be near. He knew now who this boy was; he could not doubt. But why had the baby been left behind? The king's wives had been scattered long since, and unless the boy had been left for fostering —

yes, that must have been it. But what was this thing clutching at his heartstrings?

"Bah goss!" he muttered slowly, his hand on the sleepy little fellow's curls. "Bah goss! Ah'm one ver' beeg dam fool, mebbe. Mais, she'll not be find hees fam'ly now, mebbe, Ah'm t'ink me. Alec, you's be de dam fool all de tam, so he's make no difference dis tam. You's got de shack, you's make for catch de siscowet, de muskrat, de beavair. You's got de rifle, you's make for teach dis fellair for be your son — bah goss! You's be de dam fool, Alec Brosseau — all right, den!"

With which essentials of his philosophy Alec rose, tenderly plucking little Sound-asleep up to his shoulder, and, with silent moccasins, treaded his way through moonlight and shadow toward the harbor.

There was none to hinder him, for all hands were either carousing in the log castle or plundering the farms farther inland. Alec, who had picked out an excellent Mormon canoe as his share of things, coolly visited the piles of loot which already cumbered the long wharf, selected what he fancied most, and when he had a respectable load in his canoe he put the still-sleeping boy in the bow, wrapped in one of King Strang's royal crimson robes, and shoved out.

He paddled easily, powerfully, as one used to the task. The lighthouse winked at him as he rounded the schooner's bulk, and the moonlight streamed on the open lake in front. Alec Brosseau, who had loved no man and who hated only the Irish, gazed at the huddle of golden curls forward and sang as his paddle swung up and down. He loved to sing, and men who knew him best whispered that he made his own songs — a thing which in those earlier days was no great disgrace in the timber camps.

"If you's be de king's son," he muttered suddenly, breaking off his song, "den Ah t'ink me some day we give dat dam McCurdy hell. But non — non — Ah'm not say not'ing. Jus' wait an' see. Mebbe you jus' be son to de ol' Alec Brosseau, oui!"

And disdaining to run to the shelter of the mainland, the voyageur drove out of Saint James to the east and Arbre Croche, his canoe a little black speck that bobbed on the waters and vanished. And behind him the night fell cloak-wise on the kingdom of the dispossessed.

CHAPTER II
HOW FATE FELL A-WEAVING

Cross Village, which superseded the older French settlement of Arbre Croche, lies across from Beaver Island. Then comes the northern sickle sweep of coast and the long pull obliquely across the Straits of Point Labarbe, and on five miles farther to Mackinac. Away down to the south, sixteen miles around the coast from Cross Village, lay Little Traverse — to be later known as Harbor Springs. So much for geography, which is of little moment save as it affects the destiny of men; a county or a kingdom, a farmyard or a delta, a box of earth or a seacoast — destiny works through them all alike.

The years had brought change to Michigan since the raiders had swept bare the isle of saints. Some few Mormons yet lingered in the mainland woods, now that some semblance of law sat upon the heights to protect them; the grim old judge who all but broke Schoolcraft's heart by changing the county names from Chippewa to Irish had passed beyond all Celtic jealousy; the day of voyageur and hunter had passed also, and the French had been pushed into the north whence they had come.

Into the woods had surged the Irish, rough of hand and ax, bearing with them the right of might. Here and there alone had the elder generation held its ground. Beaver Island owned a new king now, and King McCurdy acknowledged no law from the mainland even as King Strang had known none. Men muttered and whispered, but the Beavers were solidly Irish.

Not so Mackinac. The old island held grimly to its traditions and was not yet emerging into the light of tourist trade and traffic. Under the cliff cowered the village with its two streets; up the vine-clad cliff zigzagged the white trail to the fort; out beyond the cliff was the open water, across which the canoes had not yet entirely ceased to come with their furs.

In the center of town, the old Astor House still gripped the life of the North, though the Campeau store and saloon by the wharf had broken down monopoly and the brave old days were gone for good. Out in the sun beside the saloon, smoking their clay pipes and watching the color-changing water over the reef, sat the elder generation, talking little until fiery Canada West had loosened their tongues to reverie.

"Yes, we come up to make for trade," observed old Alec, blinking gravely as he chatted with Marc Groscap, who had also come in that morning by canoe from Aux Chenes to the north. "Siscowet? *Mais non!* Pelts. De boy, she's be up at de ol' post now. No, we come on de schoonair — Ah'm soon be too ol' for paddle no more, bah goss! Dat dam McCurdy, he's put in at de village. De boy, she's say, 'Hurr-ee, Alec! We go to Mackinac on de schoonair an' trade.' So Ah'm get ma pipe. De boy, she's get de pelts. We come."

Alec replaced his pipe and puffed sententiously, in unison with Marc Groscap. Old Alec Brosseau's face was deeply lined with years, and his thin hair was gray, but the old muscles were still quick and strong, though the winters had shrunken him. For half an hour neither man spoke, merely looking over the wharf and smoking, until Groscap knocked out his pipe and yawned.

"Huh! It's a fine day, Alec. See dat mist over Mackinaw way? Dat mist looks like de mirage over de Beaver, one day. You remember dat day, Alec? When we all came down to Arbre Croche wid de rifle, an' de *Able* wid Cap Wagley, an' —"

"Bah goss, you shut up!" Alec glanced around sharply, keenly, for an instant losing his pose of *le vieux* which he so loved to assume. "Ah'm t'ink me some dam Irish come along, make for scrap."

"You're the one to shut up," rejoined the swarthy Groscap, with a chuckle. "You will talk too much about dat 'dam McCurdy' some of dese days, Alec. Me, I say not'ing. You drink de w'isky too much, Alec." He suddenly lowered his voice and leaned forward, one hand tapping at the other's knee. "Alec! We ain't seen each oder for five, six year, eh? But I've not forgot, no. Mebbe you remember what you tell me one time, 'bout dat boy of yours, eh?"

"Sure." Alec nodded, nervously wiped his chin, and his eyes blinked around in caution. "Ah'm trus' you, Marc, but Ah'm not tol' nobody else. She's be de ver' fine fellair, dat boy. Bah goss! She's make de stor-ee, de chanson, all de tam; she's read in de book, she's tell me 'bout queer t'ings, she's talk to de birds, Ah'm t'ink. But she's be de good fishair, de good jack, de good axman, all de same. Ah'm 'fraid when Ah'm look at dat boy."

"Alec!" and now Groscap lowered his voice to a whisper. "Does he know, eh? You tell who his fader is, mebbe? An' how we went from Arbre Croche over to de islands —"

"Non — non!" Alec waved his hand irritably, looking out at the bay with troubled eyes. "Ah'm not say nothing, Marc. Ah'm not tell him not'ing."

"What? Does de boy t'ink you're his fader?"

"Non! Ah'm not say dat, Marc. Lissen, Marc. One day dat boy, she's get ver' curious. Ah'm say dat long tarn ago she's come to de shack, dat she's be los' in de woods, mebbe. Ah'm say dat Ah'm not know her fader, her modair, an' dat's de truth, Marc. *Ah'm not know.* Mebbe ol' Alec t'ink, but she's not *know.* Huh! What you make for do dis wintair, Marc?"

With not a change in his level voice, old Alec swiftly jumped from the subject, as a shadow struck around the corner of the log building.

"Timber camp," answered Marc briefly. "Peeling logs in de summer. I hear dat —"

The shadow became a man. He wore the high-laced leggings and short trousers which the Irish had brought into the woods, but his flannel shirt was scarlet and his boots were moccasins, and he wore no broad-rimmed, black hat. Instead, his head was bare. A mass of clear, red-gold hair glimmered in the sun, with a face below it such as seldom came out of the north woods, or into them.

Jim Brosseau, as he was known across the peninsula, was to the best of his own and Alec's knowledge about twenty-two years of age, and the hard woods and water life had touched him lightly.

High of brow and long of chin, with flexible, thin-lipped mouth and strong nose, his face was most distinctive in the eyes. They were strange, those eyes of the young lumberjack — luminous and green at times, hard, sea gray at other times, and again shifting with changing moods from gray to green. For the rest, the pull of ax and the push of paddle, the haul of nets and the stroke of peavey — all these had worked their will on his body, and had wrought it into a machine at whose perfection men marveled, which in the north woods is a rare thing.

"You'd better go up to the post, Alec," he said, his voice deep and well poised. They called each other by their first names, these two, being partners to the full. "I've picked out the grub and other things I want, so you get your pile. I'll take a stroll around and then get it packed down to the schooner. Hello, Mark Groscap! Haven't seen you for years! Where you working?"

As he gripped the swart woodsman's hand, Jim Brosseau was very good to look upon in his unassumed eagerness. Groscap stared him in the eye a moment, shook hands, turned pale, and sat down again to his pipe before replying.

"Up in Shea's camps, by Brevort. Mebbe I come sout' nex' winter, eh? Ol' Antoine Macfarlan, is he still boss at Camp Kegomic?"

"Yes," smiled Jim, knowing well what was in the other's mind, "and he keeps the Irish out of his camp, too! I've been working over there most of the winter, and after a couple more weeks I may go down to the mills at Little Traverse, or else Alec and I will go to fishing. You'd better show up next fall. There's no one to keep the peace, now, that old Père Weikamp is feeble, and there are some grand fights at the village when the French and Irish come into town!"

Alec chuckled in a rather senile fashion. He had lived so hard a life that at very occasional periods he was apt to show his age.

"Dat's been right, Marc! You come, you see ver' good scrap, mebbe! Dis little fellair, he's been lick dem dam Irish t'ree, four tam already; when Antoine's cam' come down to de village, dem Irish make for go fish, quick. Le p'tit Jim, she's be de boss scrappair from here to de Charlevoix, she's —"

"Up to the store with you, Alec," laughed Jim, flushing slightly. "The steamer will be in soon, and you've been anxious for a sight of McCurdy's girl, you know."

Alec rose and departed. Jim was turning also when Groscap rose swiftly and caught at his arm. His swarthy, wrinkled face was suddenly set in quick alarm.

"Jim! I hear dat McCurdy's come for meet his daughter from de convent at de Sault. Let me tell you dis one t'ing, Jim Brosseau. You keep 'way from dat girl — you hear me?"

The laughing, gray-green eyes met his black ones like a stab.

"Marc, I've no intention of going near her. But what right have you to order me around?"

"Right?" burst out Groscap hotly, "I've got de *knowledge,* Jim! Mebbe dat McCurdy find out who you are, den he say, 'Go kill dat man Jim.' You keep 'way from —"

Jim seized his shoulder in a fierce grip, his face suddenly tense.

"Marc, who am I, then? What do you mean by those words?"

The old woodsman suddenly shrank into himself.

"I'm de ol' fool, Jim," he muttered. "You keep quiet —"

His voice died away abruptly as steps sounded and two other men walked around the rear of the building, evidently aiming for the saloon. They both gave Groscap a keen glance, nodded pleasantly enough to Jim, and passed on.

What McCurdy's first name was, none of those around him knew. "King" McCurdy he was called, as had been King Strang before him; more often than not he was hailed as "king," accepting the name in his usual simple manner. He was an iron man, this Irishman who brooked no rival in the North. Beetling brows and thick, grizzled hair, star-bright blue eyes and steel-jaw mouth and chin, every line of his features and burly frame was vibrant with mastery and force of character. Yet he was simple in his ways; tilled his own farms on Beaver Island, wrecked ships himself, smuggled Canada West and T. & B. tobacco from the Sault himself, and it was whispered that Mary

McCurdy was coming home to a hard place after her years spent in convent and school amid gentler people and customs.

The man with McCurdy was very different. He was the mate of McCurdy's topsail schooner, the *Mary*. He was of the "red" and not the "black" Irish — lean and freckled, wiry with steel muscles, keen-eyed and thin-lipped. Tom Gallegan was twenty-five, a hard man with his fists, and was regarded as the logical candidate to succeed King McCurdy when the latter resigned from his iron rule, should that time ever come.

"You'd better come south with us, Marc," and Jim abandoned the former trend of talk after the two had passed. "Spring's nearly over, and you and I can spend the summer at Camp Kegomic —"

"Dere will be trouble," snapped Groscap, frowning and unheeding the words. "I don't like me dis Gallegan, Jim. He's got de bad eye."

He fell silent, stuffing his pipe full again and gazing out over the water. Seeing that he was in a black mood, Jim turned away and was not stopped this time.

Passing to the front of the log saloon and Campeau store, he heard loud talk and stamping of feet from inside, where a fiddle was scratching away. The crew of the *Mary* was "going" it, and Jim strode on with a frown toward the old Astor House, which stood in the center of the village — a frame building with broad veranda. Here there was an independent store whose goods were cheaper than Campeau's.

Inside he found Alec gossiping with the trader, having completed his bargains. After a few words, Jim picked up the purchases, which made a heavy load, and carried them down to the wharf. Just beyond this lay Groscap's canoe drawn up on the sand. At sight of the patched birch-and-cedar craft, Jim set down his load with a grin.

"I'll put the stuff here," he muttered. "If Marc goes home with me, I'll help him paddle; if not, I can stow the stuff aboard the schooner later on."

He turned over the canoe, loaded in the sacks, covered them with Marc's blankets, and, with a last glance at the schooner, left the wharf. On the horizon was a faint smudge of smoke, and Jim knew that Mary McCurdy would soon arrive. He felt a distaste for meeting her, perhaps bred of Marc's words, yet the enmity between French and Irish was latent. The schooner touched often at Cross Village, peddling smuggled goods or loading with honest wares, and Jim had often worked aboard her for his passage to Mackinac.

Naturally, drunken fights were frequent, but McCurdy had so far kept his men well out of any general mêlée. Antoine Macfarlan had made Camp Kegomic the last rally place of the older generation, the last point of resistance. He allowed no Irish in his camp, and when his men went to Cross Village or Little Traverse with their pay, there was sure to be a rousing fight with men from other camps or with "dock wallopers" from the mills. Therefore, Macfarlan's camp was looked upon as the nucleus of the failing French woodsmen.

Jim Brosseau passed up through the town, seeking solitude. He loved the old place, with its whitewashed or weather-stained buildings and stone chimneys, and the blazing color of hollyhocks or thorn apples scattered between. Here, through uncounted generations, had come breeds and Indians, by canoe in summer and dog sled in winter, moccasined voyageurs in gaudy sash and fur cap, lonely frontiersmen with takes of fur and fish. They would come no more. The old day was gone for all time, and the men of the old breed had died out or were hidden in far retreats where they could die in the peace they loved.

With the tin belfry of the abandoned church falling behind him, Jim climbed the white trail to the heights, avoided the fort with its soldiery, and passed on to a quiet clump of singing firs. Flinging himself down in the coarse grass, he pulled out paper and pencil, lighted his pipe, and fell to work at his writing.

He had received only one definite form of education from old Alec, consisting of lessons in rude verse which the old voyageur made with more zest than art. But the boy had been a natural poet, and the man had come to a heritage of keen nature love and keener craving for expression. Père Weikamp still lived at the half-ruined Arbre Croche monastery, which had not quite fallen into its eternal slumber, and from the wrinkled old Dutch-French Franciscan Jim had gained books and no small store of learning. Père Weikamp, the first and last of those who served beneath the old stone cross on the hill — whence the village had taken its new name — was now waiting for his end, his tomb ready built; but he had given many spiritual things to Jim Brosseau.

Of late Jim's verse had taken on rather polished accents. He did not pose, either to himself or his neighbors. In fact, no one knew of his talent save Alec, Antoine, and a choice circle at Camp Kegomic. Jim had no ambition other than to live his life in the woods among those whom he understood and who understood him — and, perhaps, to some day discover his real name and family.

So, perched on the heights above the harbor, he labored and enjoyed himself hugely. He saw the steamer come in and heard the yells of McCurdy's men, and knew that the king's daughter had come ashore. That fact touched him lightly save to draw a sudden ironic wrinkle about his eyes.

"Good thing the king left Leny behind," he chuckled. "It might have given the girl a shock to find that class of woman first crack — and on her dad's boat!"

Lena Rath, or Leny, as she was universally known, was a highly beautiful damsel originally from the garish lights of Traverse City, but now of Beaver Island. More often than not she lived aboard the schooner; at other times she visited the mainland towns or wandered farther afield, plying every trade from smuggler to charmer, loving no man yet loved of many. King McCurdy did not like her aboard his schooner, but the finest steel is that which bends most, and he knew when to bend to his men. On this trip Leny herself had been the first to recognize the necessity of keeping clear of the king's daughter.

"There's some celebration on, all right," and Jim frowned as the drunken yells lifted to him. "I've a good notion to make Marc go south and take Alec with us, to keep away from that gang. I hope Alec stays away from the mess down yonder!"

It did not occur to him that smuggled whisky was cheap, and that Alec might even then be touching hands with destiny.

CHAPTER III
UPON AN UMBER WARP

There was high celebration at Mackinac Island that day.

While the steamer was unloading its freight, the king's daughter stood on the wharf receiving homage. She was a slender, "beautiful slip of a girl," as Gallegan termed her, with something of King McCurdy's character in her glance and with his own blue eyes and black hair and red cheeks.

At first she had shrunk from the crowd — twenty-odd men having come up from the islands to greet her, and most of them half drunk by this time. But so hearty and sincere were they, so respectful were their looks and words as the king introduced them one by one, that her first shrinking passed abruptly. She was no prude, and had not known what to expect. Many of the men, indeed, she had known in her earlier years.

"Sure, they're all drunk," laughed McCurdy proudly, "but it's in your honor they're drunk, my dear! And they'll be sober for many a long day after this, mind."

Marc Groscap still sat on the beach outside the saloon, watching the scene on the wharf. Meantime, Alec Brosseau had come down from the store to rejoin him, but paused outside the saloon and turned in. It was empty except for a drunken Indian in the corner, and he flung a coin on the bar with a single word.

"Nothin' doin' today, Alec," and the bartender shoved the coin back as he set out a bottle and glass. "The king's opened the place —"

"Ah'm not drink on de king," growled Alec, pausing. "Ah'm make for pay mahself, oui! Ah'm not drink on dat dam McCurdy!"

The other looked at him, saw he was in earnest, and took the money. Alec drank, drank again, bought a half-pint flask, and went out as the first of the returning crowd sauntered up from the wharf.

At one time Alec had been able to drink the fiery Canada West like water. But that day was past, though he did not know it. He wandered forth among the bushes, seated himself on a sand dune by a clump of pine on the shore west of town, and applied himself to his flask. Before it was half gone, he was mildly intoxicated.

It was at this juncture that his mind began to dwell upon Jim. Then it occurred to him to recite some of his own compositions, which he did in no uncertain tones. Between times he finished off the flask. When he could think of no more verses to recite, he remembered that he had one of Jim's poems in his pocket.

With this thought still struggling for coherence within his brain, he heard the sound of feet, and suddenly found himself surrounded by half a dozen of the *Mary's* crew, who had also followed the trail along the shore in more or less of a maudlin state. Alec was much farther gone than they, however, and showed it.

"Bah goss!" he cried, swinging to his feet and facing around unsteadily. "Ah'm t'ink me —"

"Hello, Alec! Have a drink!" broke in one of the men, with rough good nature. Alec forgot his animosity, and instantly found himself the center of attention. He was famed as a storyteller when "primed," and every one was in mellow good humor and ready to hear tales of the old days.

"Give us a story, Alec!" cried a voice.

"Sure ye'll not mind a bit of a tale?" wheedled another. "Tell us how the Injun rigimints did be goin' to the big war, lad!"

Alec blinked around with all his innate love of theatricals aroused to the full. His last coherent thought was still struggling feebly. It was something about Jim, but he was not sure just what.

"Wait a bit; here comes Gallegan!" exclaimed one of the men.

"Ah'm make for tell you dis stor-ee," blurted Alec, paying no attention. Gallegan joined the group, lurching a little as he walked. "He's be de ver' dam fine stor-ee 'bout de ol' tam. Ah'm be work on de gov'ment ship den. Ma frien' Bedfort, she's come down from Mackinac. She's be hear dat King Strang she —"

He paused, coughing. He did not see Gallegan's swiftly uplifted hand, did not notice the sudden silence that had fallen at the name of Strang.

"Dis King Strang, she's be de bad man," he went on, after a moment. "She's take Bedfort's wife. Bedfort comes on de boat at Mackinac an' Ah'm give him ma rifle. When we get to de Saint James we tie up at de dock. Bimeby comes de king. She's hol' hees head ver' high, look ver' fine man. She's walk down de dock. Pretty soon. Ah'm hear a rifle go 'bang' an' de king —"

Alec broke off abruptly, his eyes fixed over the level horizon and his lips moving without sound. Some of the group had heard the story before, others had not. No one had ever known that old Alec had witnessed the murder of King Strang.

" 'Twas the takin' off of a big man, Mormon or not," said one. As by tacit consent, bottles and flasks were lifted all around. "What become o' Bedfort, Alec?"

"Ah'm not know," returned the old voyageur slowly. "Las' year Ah'm hear dat hees son, she's be run de rev'noo cuttair — but Ah'm not know not'ing."

"Sure an' that's right, boys!" cried one of the men eagerly. "The new officer in command — Leftenant Bedfort, d'ye mind? What d'ye know about that, now?"

"Shut your jaw!" commanded Gallegan quickly. "What's the cutter to us, you cursed fool!"

There was a general wink. As a matter of fact, the cutter was a good deal to the king's men.

"Come, now," said Gallegan, a bit thickly, turning to Alec. "Tell us about the time you come to the Beavers with the king, Brosseau."

"Aye, lad, do be tellin' us that!" chimed in another voice. "Tell us about the raid, an' what the king was doin' that day!"

Alec looked about. His eyes went from face to face, and he shivered a little.

"Ah'm not want for remembair dat," he declared simply. "Dat dam McCurdy, she's be de ver' bad man, oui! A long tarn ago, dis was de good country, dis. Plenty sishcawet, plenty deer, plenty voyageur. Now de dam Irish make for change all dat."

There was a moment's startled silence, followed by a short laugh. Alec's outburst was in no sense personal. He did not realize that his auditors were Irish to a man, and he was simply voicing a subconscious grievance. Nor might the group have taken any offense, save for Gallegan.

"Don't get too gay with them cuss words!" snapped out the mate, his eyes looking ugly. "This ain't any consolation meeting, Alec. You've talked too much on the Irish question, anyhow. Some day you'll get what's comin' to ye, unless ye shut up! Same to that boy Jim o' yours."

Alec caught at the word. His face lightened up.

"Ah — dat fellair Jim!" he said eagerly. "She's be de fine boy, dat! Mebbe you know dat Ah'm sometam make de chanson mahself, non? Ah'm hear de 'ping-g-g' of de ax an' Ah'm make de chanson." As he spoke, Alec began to gesture extravagantly, and the group drew closer together in amused interest.

"When Ah'm hear de flop of de fish, de click of de skidding tongs, de rip of de peavy — den Ah'm make de stor-ee, de chanson, oui! Ah'm be de good jack, me. But dat fellair Jim, she's be de bettair jack. She's get de mos' fish; Ah'm tell you somet'ing Ah'm hear. Dat fellair Jim, she's talk to de birds!"

Now in their own way the Irish lumberjacks were quite as superstitious as the older generation. This had been rather increased by the absence of religion, King McCurdy having frowned upon the return of the mission to the island. Seeing that Alec was quite in earnest, the half-drunken group drew together with an uneasy look around.

"What d'ye mean?" demanded Gallegan blackly, with a hiccup.

"Ah'm tell you dis!" answered Alec triumphantly. "Dat fellair Jim, she's make de chanson, oui! She's go out an' lie in de fores', talk to de birds, oui! Mebbeso de squirrel come by, she's see dat fellair Jim, she's go up an' say, 'B'jou, M'sso Jim!' Den dat fellair Jim she's say 'b'jou,' an' den de squirrel she's make for tell him one ver' fine chanson to give ol' Alec."

"G'wan, ye're — ye're dhrunk!" stuttered Gallegan, who fell into his brogue when in liquor. "Makes songs — the like o' him!"

"She's be de bettair man dan you!" flamed out Alec. He did not detect the savage undernote in the laugh that greeted this remark. "You dam Irish! Mebbeso you don't b'lieve what Ah'm tol' you, huh?"

Gallegan swayed a little on his feet, his cruel lips drawn back, his hard gray eyes narrowed dangerously.

"Don't believe you!" he shot out, in maudlin anger. "Talkin' to birds, is it? Faith, either you're dhrunker'n I am or else I'm dhrunker'n you, Alec Brosseau! I've a gr-rand notion to be givin' ye a remembrance —"

"Wait a bit!" broke in another, seizing his arm, "Alec, is it tellin' the thruth ye are, lad? About them birds an' squirrels, I mane."

Alec glared at them defiantly. He seemed to sense the ominous looks brought forth by his repetition of the words "dam Irish."

"You's be de dam fool," he said, with admirable generality of address. "Ah'm tol' you de trut', oui. Mebbe you nevair hear de chanson dat fellair make, huh? Den you know not'ing a-tall! You's be de dam fool."

This method of speech was not calculated to smooth the injured feelings of the men, though Alec cared little for them. Gallegan was sullenly angry, but the others were still possessed by drunken curiosity.

They continued to question Alec about his statements, and his fine air of mystery only served to add zest to their questions. Little by little he calmed down again, becoming wrapped up in his subject, but his references to McCurdy began to sting them. As he grew more docile, they took on something of Gallegan's somber rage, until finally the mate pushed through the group and faced Alec with the lie direct.

"Ye're dhrunk, ye ould fool!" roared Gallegan furiously. "Ye've been handin' us a pack o' lies! The lad niver made no poetry. He's jest the same kind of a dhreamin' fool that y'are yersilf!"

Alec, meantime, had imbibed once more from a friendly bottle. Consequently the mate's words struck only a maudlin chuckle from him. He had now remembered that scrap of paper in his pocket.

"Mebbe you nevair hear de chanson Jim make," he hiccuped, fishing in his pocket amid a mass of tangled lines, tobacco, and odds and ends. "You dam Irish! Ah'm make for show you something, huh?"

Gallegan flung up his arm with a growl of rage, but one of the other men caught him back. They were all too eager to know if there had been truth in Alec's statements. If so, it was easy to see where Jim Brosseau would have the verse-making deviled out of him ere long. It had been his own secret; now it was passing into other hands, though Alec's boasting recked naught of this.

"You got a poem there?" inquired one of the men, with a leer. "Read her off, ol' hoss!"

"Ah'm make for fin' it," muttered Alec as he searched. Then with a cry of triumph he drew forth the dirty scrap of paper and held it up.

Alec was particularly proud of that verse, because Jim had written it expressly to appeal to the old man. It had nothing of himself in it; it was for Alec pure and simple, and Alec appreciated it. Also, Antoine Macfarlan and the chosen circle at Camp Kegomic had appreciated its general sentiment. What was more, certain lines of it had been quoted more than once in saloons at Little Traverse and Cross Village, had spread farther into other camps, and were causing fights from Boyne City to Mackinac.

The verse in its entirety had never bean heard beyond Camp Kegomic, however. It is quite certain Jim had never looked forward to its popularity, for it was nothing of which he was in the least proud. The pride of old Alec had been held in to the bursting point, but whisky had now loosened the jam and was destined to do worse. There was a swing to the words that had fascinated the hearers before this, and with proud anticipation Alec held up his scrap of paper and looked around.

"Now you keep ver' quiet," he warned the grinning men sternly. "Ah'm make for read you dis chansom what dat fellair Jim she's wrote, oui!"

And so he read it, unheeding the black growl that broke out with the first line from those around. As the thing had been written in his own dialect, he was able to do it all the more justice.

"Oh, Jean le Longue hees arm be strong
An' he's take hees w'isky clear!
He's buck de jam an' he's fight de cam',
An' he's make for look for de dam — dam — dam —

Dam McCurdy, an' skin hees han'
When he's drive de Irish from Michigan!
An' he's lay de king on de barroom floor
But Jean le Longue he's look for more,
For he's take hees w'isky clear
By gar!
He's take hees w'isky clear!"

Alec paused, and glanced around for approbation. He received none. The ominous silence failed to warn him, for he was chuckling to himself in entire forgetfulness of these listeners.

"G'wan wid it," growled a hoarse voice. Gallegan was breathing hard, and there was murder in his face.

"She's be de ver' fine chanson, huh?" chuckled Alec fatuously, and he hummed a bar of the rough air which had been fitted to the verse. Gallegan's fists were clenched, and his face went white. That air was getting known even at the Beavers. Holding up his paper again, Alec continued:

"Oh, Jean le Longue hees arm be strong
An' he's take hees w'isky clear!
He's look for tight from morn to night,
An' he's put de calks to de Irishman!
He's bus' de jail at Pierre le Gran',
He's lose one eye an' hees ear's been tore,
But hees fis' she's split dat — big — jail — door,
An' de Irish run when he's look for more.
For he's take hees w'isky clear,
By gar!
He's take hees w'isky clear!"

Alec blinked around with a weak grin. Even as he did so, the infuriated Gallegan tore himself free and his fist landed brutally on the old man's jaw. Alec spun around with a choking cry.

He tried to fight, but he was given no chance. The half dozen men were out of their heads with whisky and rage, and all the brutish passion of the north woods was unleashed in them. They drove in smashing blows, hitting each other and Alec without discrimination, a frenzy of blood lust upon them all.

Alec went to his knees, groaning, his hands feebly held before him. Gallegan gripped him about the neck and held him up, sending over his right to the old man's blood-streaked mouth. Then the broken voyageur went limp, and fell.

But Gallegan was not through, for he had been bred in the woods and was used to the utter brutality of woods ethics. True, he had no calks on his boots, but he went savagely at the limp figure with both feet, stamping and kicking. Even his men were horrified, and attempted to pull him off. They did not succeed, but an instant later came a quiet voice behind them that caused Gallegan to pause and whirl around abruptly.

"Well, boys? What's going on?"

King McCurdy stood looking at them, with a glint in his ice-blue eyes that made the others shrink back to leave Gallegan facing him. Then for the first time McCurdy saw the body of Alec, and his face flamed slowly.

"What's goin' on, is it?" returned Gallegan thickly and unabashed, his breast heaving. "The ould un here was —"

The king had seen enough, however, and desired to hear nothing.

"Ye born fools!" he broke out, terrible anger in his deep voice. "To the dock wid ye!"

He waited not to be obeyed, but his fist shot out, and Gallegan went down. The king made one leap and was among the others, striking right and left with blows that would leave their mark for many a day. As they broke before him he flung a glance at Alec's form, shook his head, and moved away toward town.

Behind him trailed the others, lurching over the brown sand, while Gallegan nursed a split mouth with many curses. The big, uncouth figures wound in among the scattered birch and pine after the dominant McCurdy; then they were lost from sight, reappeared, and finally vanished among the houses.

Behind them, in among the clump of pine and bushes, old Alec's battered visage looked up to the blue sky. Despite its blood and bruises the face was peaceful. Its wrinkles seemed to have fallen away of a sudden; in one hand was still clenched a scrap of dirty paper, in among the sparse locks of gray hair ventured a sand spider, and over the faded and torn blue shirt wandered a big ant, darting back from the flecks of blood.

An hour passed. The sun was westering, and only the whisper of waves from the shore below broke the peace of the Northland. Then, without warning, the bushes parted. Through them stepped Jim Brosseau.

CHAPTER IV
HOW A POET SOUGHT JUSTICE

Jim had lived a rough life enough, but he was very much of a boy, and still more of a dreamer. He knelt over Alec, sobbing unrestrainedly, clasping the gray head to his breast.

His trained eye had told him the whole story. The footprints in the sand, the bottles and flasks, the scrap of paper clenched in Alec's fingers — he needed no more than these to reconstruct what had happened here. A flicker of life in the broken body stirred him out of his grief, however.

Catching up one of the flasks, he ran down to the shore and filled it hurriedly with water. When this had been emptied over Alec's face a cry of joy broke from the younger man; the voyageur's lids opened, and Alec groaned faintly.

"Bah goss!"

"Keep quiet, Alec!" cried Jim softly, tears still wet on his cheeks. The old man was looking up vacantly, but when he met the gray-green eyes his own cleared suddenly. He groaned again.

"Dey got me, Jim;" he breathed.

"Ah'm — go de las' trail —"

A tear fell on his cheek. The warm touch seemed to give him strength, and there was unbounden love in the faded eyes that looked up to Jim's face.

"Don't cry," he muttered feebly. "Jim, dat dam Gallegan —"

"I'll make him pay!" broke out Jim, a rush of quick rage banishing the anguish from his features as he lifted his face to the sky. "So help me, I'll —"

"Wait," broke in Alec. "Ah'm not got ver' much tarn lef', Jim. Ah'm go — de las' trail —"

"Lie back and rest," exclaimed Jim swiftly. One look into the bruised face had shown him that the end was not far. "I'll run and get the priest."

"No!" commanded Alec with more strength, and he managed a wistful smile. "Ah'm not need de good père, Jim. Ah'm got — got for tell you — one t'ing."

Sobbing again, Jim leaned over and caressed the old man. Alec shivered.

"Lissen, Jim! Ah'm tol' you dat Ah'm not know your fader. She's be de one — de one ver' beeg lie —" He paused, fighting desperately for life.

"Ah'm fin' you at de Beavair, Jim — de day we drove de Mormon — Jim! Jim!" His voice suddenly gathered strength, rose to a wild cry, "Jim! Ah'm make for lie to you! You's be de son — de son of de ol' king — you's be de son —"

He choked, fell back, and lay quiet. The peace of the North had come upon him.

Now that he knew Alec dead beyond any doubt, Jim's grief mastered him. The tears did him good, afforded him an outlet, and gradually allowed a clearheaded sanity to drift in upon his brain. When he had sobbed himself dry-eyed he suddenly realized that the sun was almost perched upon the horizon, a glowing ball of red. Slightly to the south of it lay a shadow over the waters — the mirage of the Beavers.

Slowly Jim lifted his head, staring at the failing sun. His red-gold hair flew glittering in the breeze, his thin-lipped, strong mouth still quivered somewhat, his eyes were now a hard and cold sea gray, and as they rested on the cold dead shoulders his powerful hands were clenched until the knuckles stood up white.

The call to vengeance wakened within him, a flame of fury quickening in his eyes and rousing him to action. He rose, his whole stern-lined face set and grim and cold; for he knew whom to seek, and where.

"You, Tom Gallegan!" His deep, musical voice rang out as if the man himself were standing there facing him. "You shall pay for this — pay! If I do not see you hung at Charlevoix, may God curse you! And first, I'll meet you man to man and down you, and roll you, and put the calks to you — oh, God, God! To murder old Alec — poor old Alec!"

With a sob he stooped and lifted the body in his arms easily. The splendid power of his body showed no sign of effort or fatigue as he strode across the sand, following in the tracks left by McCurdy and his men. He did not hurry, for he knew this vengeance could not escape him.

He was no more the dreamer, the poet; he was the lumberjack, roused to a wild craving after payment in kind for his injuries. Before he got into the town, men and women were already watching him; as he passed the Astor House the group by the door stared at him in mild surmise. Jim paid no heed to them, nor to the voices lifting and calling after him. He strode on toward the wharf, never caring for the picture he must have presented, every nerve in his body quivering with fierce anger.

Head flung back, eyes blazing, with Alec's gray hair drooping from the limp head across his shoulder, he passed the Campeau store and barroom, and set foot on the wharf. Marc Groscap still sat by the side wall of the saloon, but Jim did not turn to glance at him. His eyes were fastened on the schooner in front; the steamer had pulled out long since.

News of his coming had passed ahead, for he could see the men pouring up on deck and joining the group that stood on the wharf. In front of them was King McCurdy, legs planted wide, hands in jacket pockets, face dour and grim. Until he met the keen blue eyes beneath their shaggy brows, Jim had never doubted of getting that which he sought.

Now, however, he felt a sudden hesitation which was borne down instantly by a new wave of anger. He knew better than to appeal to law here at Mackinac against any man of the king's own. If he wanted justice, he would have to seek it from McCurdy — and he was savagely determined to have justice. Nor was the king likely to deny it, he considered. McCurdy had the name of maintaining a rude authority and a ruder justice, yet except for those aboard wrecked vessels, which was no more than rumor, murder was a thing not told against him.

McCurdy waited in grim silence, the crowd behind him grouped together in sullen apprehension, Gallegan at his elbow. In that instant Jim felt hate in his heart for all these men. He remembered Alec's tales and constant mutter against the Irish; he sensed himself as one of the older race; he could feel the subtle tie of blood which banded them against him and set their eyes in sullen antagonism, Gallegan was perfectly sober by this time, and his face was terribly pale. Even in the north woods murder of white men was a thing well avoided.

Jim strode on, and paused two yards from McCurdy. Tenderly he bent down and lowered his burden to the rough planks; at sight of the body Gallegan's features went ghastly, and those who had been with him drew farther back into the crowd. With a terrible calm settled upon him, Jim rose and faced King McCurdy. Behind, at the edge of the wharf, had gathered a little group of town loafers. Marc Groscap was standing before his bench, staring wildly.

"I want justice, McCurdy!" snapped out Jim bluntly, fighting down the rage that swirled into him at sight of Gallegan. "Your mate there murdered Alec this afternoon. I demand that you throw Gallegan in irons and take him to Charlevoix for trial."

McCurdy's eyes roved over the splendid figure of the young woodsman. It was said that the king always loved a man who could face him without fear, and certain it was that he read no fear in Jim's face. His own was like stone.

"What, lad — is he dead?" There was a soft note of unwonted pity in McCurdy's voice which only lashed Jim the more. "That is a bad charge to make against a man, Jim. What proof have ye?'"

"Proof!" cried out Jim, his voice ringing like a bell. "Proof! You have a heel off your right boot, King McCurdy. I saw your tracks where Alec lay. Give me justice or I charge *you* with the murder!"

At this McCurdy himself was taken aback. He did not see the figure standing by the after-deck house aboard the schooner, nor did Jim.

"Come, lad; come!" exclaimed McCurdy, his deep voice stirred into its usual cold dominance. "Did ye see Gallegan's tracks, too?"

"No," Jim flung back at him challengingly. "But Alec told me who killed him before he — died. It was brutal work, McCurdy — for that red-eyed dog of yours to put the boots to an old man like Alec! Will you give me justice or not?"

McCurdy looked at him steadily. The sun was all but gone, and a smell of cooking drifted over the group from the schooner's galley.

"It'll be a hard thing to prove, I'm thinkin'," came his answer slowly. "Ye have but a dead man's word for it, Jim —"

"His word dead is better than yours living," cried Jim hotly, struggling with his overmastering rage. He flashed a look at Gallegan which made the mate step back suddenly. "So help me, McCurdy, either you give him over to the law or —"

The tense situation was suddenly relieved in most unexpected fashion. From the rail jumped a girl, pushing through the group.

"Father! What does all this mean? Surely Mr. Gallegan —"

"Mary!" King McCurdy whirled as though struck. "Get below where you belong!"

For answer the girl merely looked at him, and he gave back before the scorn in her eye. She turned, and Jim had his first sight of Mary McCurdy. She was tall, almost to his own height, and above her head was coiled a mass of bronze-black hair that fell low upon her neck to the brown convent dress below. At sight of her face, however, Jim felt a sudden thrill of wonder shoot through him.

She had her father's features, almost line for line — black brows, strong nose, sea-blue eyes, a mouth and chin which spelled character. Yet every feature was changed. The brows were fine and almost penciled, contrasting strongly with the red Irish cheeks of her; the nose was thin and sensitive, the eyes strangely wistful and searching, the mouth and chin rounded into curves of womanly beauty that almost hid the strength beneath.

"Who is this man?" she inquired, and her face paled at sight of Alec's body. "Is it true what he says, father?"

McCurdy tried to speak, but Jim forestalled him.

"True!" and the bitterness in his voice drew the girl's eyes again to his face. "Look at this old man — look at Gallegan! Do you need more proof?"

Gallegan tried to gather himself, but failed utterly.

"Who are you?" demanded the girl again, her eyes striking Jim's steadily.

"None of your business, girl," shot out McCurdy. "For the love of Hiven will ye get below before I'm takin' ye there?"

"I will not!" She faced him squarely, twisting away from his extended hand. "Is this charge true, father? Do you shelter murderers?"

McCurdy looked into her eyes — and turned away with a muttered oath.

"Sure, it's not true at all!" cried a voice behind. "Tell 'em so, Tom!"

"Yes, tell *me* so!" Jim caught at the word and whirled on Gallegan, a cold flame dancing in his eyes. "Tell me so, you murderer! Say it, if you dare!"

"You're drunk!" whispered Gallegan, then pulled himself together. He had been badly shaken, but he was neither coward nor fool, and now swift, anger leaped into his face. "It's a black lie!" he stormed out.

There was a moment of silence, while the girl looked from one to the other. Gallegan lost his assurance when he tried to meet Jim's gaze. McCurdy had been swiftly shoved into the background momentarily.

"Sure," spoke up a man from behind. "Tom didn't do it, lad! Wasn't he wid us all afthernoon? How'd he be doin' the like o' that now?"

A chorus of assent welled up from the others. The young woodsman took no heed, but fastened his eyes on Gallegan. Before the indomitable purpose in those gray-green depths, before their lambent flame of revenge, the mate shifted uneasily, and his keen eyes fell. They shifted again from Alec's body, and Gallegan stared at his boots.

"Who are you?" asked the girl for the third time.

Jim looked at her stonily.

"Ask your father," he returned in a hard voice "Ask your father, the man who shields murderers, who looks on and sees murder done on an old man, who tries to lie out of it afterward! Ask *him* who I am, Mary McCurdy."

At this juncture, however, King McCurdy once more leaped into command of the situation. Old Marc Groscap was advancing slowly up the wharf, with a few bolder townsfolk behind him.

"Go keep them fools back!" ordered the king savagely. Four of his men pushed past Jim, shrinking a little from the body of Alec. Jim heard Mate's voice raised in anger, heard a scuffle, but paid no attention.

"Now see here, Jim Brosseau," began McCurdy without further parley. "This story of yours is a pack o' lies, that's all. Tom didn't do this dirty work. He's been uptown with me all day, and I ain't been out where you said Alec was killed —"

"I didn't say," snapped out Jim dryly. "How did you know where it was?"

Silence fell. McCurdy's face turned a deep red, for the contempt in the woodsman's voice was stinging. A slow, horrified wonder crept into the girl's eyes, and she turned swiftly on Gallegan.

"Did you kill this old man?" she demanded. "Answer me! Did you?"

"I did not," returned the mate stoutly taking heart.

"And what if he did?" broke in McCurdy swiftly, his blue eyes incisive with the anger that rose in him "You clear out of here, Jim, and do it quick. Go get the law if ye want, an' see what it does for ye! Go get some kind o' proof, an' then come back —"

Jim, white-faced with desperate fury, played his last card.

"All right, McCurdy!" he exclaimed savagely, taking a step forward. "I'll take Tom's word that he's innocent — on one condition."

"Well — what is it?"

"That he step over here and touch Alec's body."

A dead silence fell again. Every man there knew what Jim meant — it was the old superstition that if the murderer touched his victim, the latter's wounds would reopen. The issue was put squarely up to Tom Gallegan, and every eye sought the mate.

He stared at Jim, his strong, hard-lined face dark in the gathering twilight. Bitterly did he regret killing Alec in his drunken madness, but the thing was done, and, next to McCurdy himself, Gallegan was the strongest man present in Irish eyes. He made a gallant effort to prove his strength, and without a sound stepped he was standing over Alec's body.

"Stoop down and touch him!" commanded Jim abruptly. "He's dead."

The word lashed Gallegan like a blow. He leaned over and reached out a tentative hand toward Alec's bruised face — then jerked up with his own face as ghastly as that of the dead man.

"Yes!" he cried out hoarsely. "I killed him, damn ye! The ould fool would be provokin' me wid his talk, and it was dhrunk we all were."

Jim looked over Gallegan's shoulder at McCurdy.

"Well?" he said, bitterness in his voice. "Will you deliver this man to justice or not, King McCurdy?"

"I will not!" roared the other angrily. "Ye've heard what he said, that Alec did be provokin' him —"

"Then I'll take justice into my own hands," cried Jim, white-lipped.

Swift as lightning, his fists shot out. Right and left smacked into Gallegan's face, and again. Even as the girl shrank away with a cry, the woodsman drove home another terrible blow that sent Gallegan reeling back into the schooner's rail with a crash.

Jim leaped after him, stark madness in his brain. McCurdy halted him with a blow, but his fist went into the king's jaw like a hammer, and McCurdy fell back. The woodsman found Gallegan staggering up, and planted one blow that drove the mate senseless to the wharf. With that the crowd closed around him.

Those nearest the schooner's rail caught out belaying pins, and with a roar the surge of maddened men swept back and forth. In the midst flew out the young woodsman's red-gold hair, for they had not rushed him off his feet and he was fighting as he had never fought before, realizing that it was for his very life. His only thought was to exact vengeance to the uttermost, and the terrific force of his blows sent men down to right and left, but others closed in upon him from every side.

Still he fought them off, and so managed to get his back to the schooner's rail. For an instant they drew back before him, then a belaying pin flickered from the rear of the crowd and struck him full across the head. He staggered, and they were on him like wolves.

Again he beat them back, but more blows landed. The pain cleared his head and made him think of safety; with a savage rush he tried to break through, failed, and reeled as another pin crashed through his guard. Back to the corner of the wharf end they forced him, and now a savage yell rose:

"Dhrown him, byes! Dhrown him!"

With the black water cutting off escape, he fought doggedly, desperately, driving his fists into the contorted, savage faces that hemmed him in and forced him ever backward. Then on a sudden there shrilled a voice to him — from behind:

"Jim! You make for jump —"

A hasty glance over his shoulder gave him a glimpse of Marc Groscap in his canoe, under the schooner's taff-rail. At the same instant the mob came at him with a wild yell. Jim paused, sent his fist crashing into the foremost face, then leaped out backward.

The icy water closed around him, shocking him into new life. He came to the surface amid a shower of belaying pins and missiles, struck out, and felt Marc's hand on his shoulder. "Over de end, Jim; over de end!" And as he sprawled into the big canoe, Jim's first coherent thought was that it was a good thing he had stowed his purchases in Marc's craft instead of the schooner. Five minutes later they were driving out into the open straits.

CHAPTER V
AND WAS GIVEN KING'S NAME
BY A STRANGER

Jim stared at the wall with somber eyes, slowly stuffing his pipe with what remained of Alec's kinnikinnick.

Everything about the old shack was sharp with torturing memories to him. In the corner was Alec's much-mended net with its floats, half hiding the old, long rifle which stood behind it, powder horn on peg. Near the fireplace were the squat snowshoes, thonged with the gut of the last deer ever Alec had shot. In the embers of the fireplace was the old battered frying pan just as Alec had left it on that morning when Jim had sighted the schooner standing in to Cross Village and had summoned him hurriedly.

The tattered newspaper cuts and cheap prints on the wall, the old double-bladed ax, the boots and clothes, the steel traps — everything was eloquent of the old voyageur who had passed on the last trail. And there were the things Jim himself had owned — the French Bible given him by Père Weikamp, a book of selected poems, a tintype Alec had had taken of him ten years before, all the odds and ends which had gathered through the long years. They were all his now.

"You get de law from Charlevoix, Jim."

Marc's last words rang in his ears still. A week before this they had landed at the creek mouth, three miles above the village, and Groscap's canoe lay there now in the bushes. Marc himself had decided that having come south for Jim's sake, he might well remain for his own; so on finding that the moody and heartbroken Jim could not be stirred from his grieving, he had departed for Camp Kegomic. It was still early spring, and there would be work in plenty.

Jim had remained, cursing himself bitterly for his futile madness that day on the wharf at Mackinac, sunk in a stupor of grief. But gradually the renewed desire for vengeance had welled up within him. He imagined that Gallegan's confession could not well be disproven, and the law would be carried to the Beavers despite King McCurdy, for the island was in Charlevoix County and at Charlevoix was a sheriff of some repute. So at length Jim's quietude had worn itself out, and with his vigorous body craving action, he had decided to tramp overland to Charlevoix and set the law to work.

After a meager breakfast he was ready. He might have gone by canoe, but had no heart for it; he craved the solitude of the woods, the companionship of trees and animal things. His route lay to Little Traverse and on around the shore to Petoskey; this would require a day, and another would take him on to Charlevoix.

So in the dawn light he set forth, taking only a little food with him. He wanted nothing from his old life until his vengeance had been satisfied; then he could return to his life and work if he so wished.

Striking down by the shore road, he avoided the village with only a glimpse at the big sunrise-red cross atop the hill. The opening of the county had flung a swarm of homesteaders around Cross Village and Little Traverse, but the Indians still gripped the best land, and not all of them were foolish enough to trade it for a mess of pottage.

With hot desire in his heart to spur him on, Jim walked faster than he knew, striding swiftly onward with his whole thought centered on what was to come. His broken head was well by this time only a red scab remaining of the cut on his brow.

Before noon he was through Little Traverse, pausing not for the greetings which met him. The tale of Alec's death was already spreading far, garbled and distorted, but Jim was in no mood to barter gossip, and pushed on unmindful around the curving shores of the bay till he struck down to the Marquette Trail and so came into the net of destiny.

Trudging steadily along the trail was an Indian. Jim recognized him as Joe Bigfoot, who carried the mails from Chiboygan to Traverse City by way of Petoskey. Joe had been in one of the Indian regiments which served in the Civil War years before, and now carried the mail week in and week out as reliably as a machine. He greeted the woodsman, nodding.

"B'jou, Jim Brosseau!"

"B'jou," smiled Jim, who knew the man and liked him. "Want company as far as Charlevoix, Joe?"

"Uh-huh! Tabac?"

Jim handed him some kinnikinnick, and Joe grunted again as he filled his pipe with the mixed willow and tobacco. On they trudged together in the silence of perfect understanding; then, still two miles out of Petoskey, they came upon a man standing in the road and evidently waiting for the mail carrier. Upon seeing them he rose and shuffled toward them in a cloud of dust.

He was a stranger to Jim, an elderly, heavily bearded, slouchily dressed man with a peculiar gleam in his sunken eyes that attracted the woodsman's attention. As they approached he held up a dirty letter.

"Hello!" he cried in a deep-chested voice. "I come down to meet ye, Joe. Will ye send off this letter for me? My wife's sick, and it'll save me goin' into town."

The Indian nodded, and took the letter with the coin handed him. Then for the first time the man seemed to see Jim. He gazed at him for a moment, and Jim could have sworn there was fear in the deep gray eyes. "Who are you?"

The question shot out with almost savage emphasis on the last word. Startled at the man's aspect, Jim looked at him keenly, but saw that he was perfectly sober.

"My name's Jim Brosseau," he smiled. The hard lines which had been graven in his face were banished before that smile, yet the frank kindliness of it seemed to strike swift wonder to the bearded farmer.

"Brosseau! Brosseau!" he repeated, while Joe Bigfoot shifted his pack impatiently. "No, it's impossible! I'm crazy!"

"You talk like it," laughed Jim, a little irritated. "Are you a stranger here?"

"Yes," broke out the other fiercely, his eyes flaring suddenly. "A stranger in the land of my fathers! A — but tell me, friend, who are you?"

"I've told you already," answered the woodsman, with a glance at Joe. "All right, Joe, I'm coming."

"Wait — wait!" The big man stopped him with extended hand, searching his face with those peculiar eyes. "Don't go yet, friend, I want to talk to you."

"Then you'll have to take another time." Jim began to think the man was really somewhat crazed, and repressed his anger. "I'm going to Charlevoix with Joe, and I've no time to waste."

"Charlevoix! And what do you there, friend?"

"Good Lord, man, is that your business or mine?" Jim's impatience broke out beyond restraint. "I'm going to Charlevoix, and from there to the Beavers —"

"Don't do it!"

At the sudden exclamation Jim stopped to search that bearded face again. What on earth could the man mean? He seemed merely a farmer from the half-cleared land back from the bay, yet there was undoubtedly something striking in his looks.

"Don't do it, friend!" he went on quickly and with an earnestness which impressed Jim despite his impatience, "If you go to the island with that face — friend, it would be suicide! You don't know those devils there!"

"I know them better than you," retorted Jim half angrily. "Get out of the way and let me by, will you? What's wrong with my face? If I need a shave that's not your affair, my friend,"

The other leaned forward swiftly, dropping his voice.

"Friend, you can't fool me, but you can trust me. Come, be frank with me! You have the king's face, the king's voice — why, man, if it was thirty years back you might be the king himself when we came to Beaver Island and took it from the Lamanites!"

The tense excitement of the man was not the only thing that roused sudden interest in Jim. In a flash he recalled those final words of Alec's — those words which he had almost forgotten, when Alec had tried to tell him who he was. For an instant he looked into the deep-sunken eyes, then turned quickly.

"Go ahead, Joe! I'll catch you at Petoskey."

The Indian grunted, and moved off. Jim turned back again, his eyes aglow.

"My friend, I don't know who you are. I don't know who I am myself. But I do know that I've been told the same thing you just hinted at — that I'm the son of a king. Do you mean by this that I'm the son —"

"Don't talk here, friend," exclaimed the man hastily. "Come home with me, and we shall converse in peace."

Jim hesitated only for a moment. He guessed swiftly from the man's words that he had been one of the Mormon settlers on Beaver Island; the thing which he half guessed sent the blood leaping through his veins, drove thought of his mission from him, and forced him into following the long strides of his new-found friend through the woods

There was only one king of whom he could be the son. The man's recognizance was startling enough, but Jim had heard that more than one of Strang's scattered band lived in the vicinity — lonely, hated men who wrestled with earth for bread, who seldom showed themselves in the dwellings of other men, remnants of the once powerful kingdom that had passed forever. He had never met one of these men before, but he had heard tales of them. There were not many of them left, and no one knew exactly where they were or who, except that they were. As a rule, they kept their religion and blood a strict secret.

Jim gave over all thought of revenge for the present. That could wait. Meantime, he was afire with the suggested thought which lay in his mind. He had never known his real name, and he had thought that Alec did not know it. Now it suddenly came to him like a shock how Alec had called him James, and why. The town of Saint James — James Strang, the apostle of Mormon —

He strode on with strange fancies flooding his brain. The older man walked ahead in silence, his matted gray beard swinging from side to side with his stride. They struck straight in from the shore to the thickly wooded heights behind, and Jim guessed they had covered a good two miles and more when his guide suddenly flung up a hand.

"There, friend, is the abode of peace and righteousness. Enter, and may blessing come upon you!"

Jim beheld a rude house of balsam logs set on a small hill. The place was wild and uncouth, and beyond it he could glimpse a stretch of cleared land with a "slashing" behind, all enclosed by the older growth of timber. The house was not a new one, and Jim calculated swiftly that his host must have come here into the woods twenty years before, at the time the Beavers were raided.

Then he stepped inside. The house comprised two rooms only, partly separated by a tattered blanket and a deerskin. The outer room was bare to austerity; slab chairs, a rough table, a few newspaper cuts tacked to the wall — this was all. The inner room held two beds, on one of which lay a gray-haired woman. She was breathing heavily, and her eyes were closed. The young woodsman knew she must be the wife of whom the Mormon had spoken.

His host glanced anxiously at her figure, jerked his matted beard, then motioned Jim to a chair, and took one himself. Pulling off his wide hat he disclosed a head nearly bald, fastened his piercing gray eyes on Jim, and spoke in a solemn tone of voice.

"Friend, do you know how the Gentiles cut off the people of King Strang, even as the people of Nephi were rooted out by the Lamanites?"

Jim, gazing at him, comprehended now that he had to deal with a fanatic, but cared little for that.

"I don't know about the last named," he answered, smiling slightly, "but I've heard about the raid on Beaver Island, of course. Alec had a hand in that himself."

"Alec!" queried the other, frowning.

Jim needed no urging, and knowing that he must be frank in order to expect frankness, told of the old voyageur and what he knew of himself. The other listened with smoldering eyes, and at the end lifted a hand toward a faded picture cut from a newspaper and tacked near the stone fireplace.

"Friend, draw near and look at that picture!"

Jim, feeling impressed despite himself, rose and examined the yellowed cut. It showed a high-browed, tight-lipped face, whiskered after an earlier fashion, yet with striking eyes of power. Beneath it was the half-defaced print, "James Strang, This Week Acquitted of Treason in —"

"Is it not written that the blood of the saints shall cry to the Lord?" exclaimed the other solemnly. "There shall be murders and robbing —"

The young woodsman heard him not, for he was gazing at the face of King Strang, wondering if this man had indeed been his father. He turned suddenly, his own face tight set.

"I've told you my story," he declared quietly, dominating the older man for the moment. "I don't know who you are my friend, but you seem to believe that I'm the son of James Strang. Now, is this so? What do you know about me?"

"God has not ceased to be a God of miracles!" returned the old Mormon, forcing himself into calm with an evident effort. "I was on the island when the Gentiles came; I put my wife into a canoe and fled hither. Not from that day to this have we known what became of our daughter Sariah, and here have we dwelt alone. But there was a young son of King James, friend — a boy, born after the death of the holy man. He also disappeared that day. And behold! After twenty years do I find him upon the highway, led of God back to the land of his fathers, knowing not his birthright!"

"And led by vengeance also!" cried Jim hotly, for while he had told of Alec's death he had said nothing of his mission at Charlevoix. Now he declared it eagerly enough, looking for approbation and encouragement.

This knowledge of himself had come so suddenly, so unexpectedly, that it put fire to his imagination and lifted him to exalted heights. He was still very much of a boy, a dreamer who had dwelt alone with the woods and knew little of men, fit timber to be shaped by the sunken-eyed fanatic who sat and watched him with kindling eyes.

In this moment the drift of years bore fruit. Jim felt he was in truth the son of James Strang, and remembered a thousand little things which went to back it up. More, he knew that Marc Groscap and Antoine Macfarlan would know — even as Alec had known and lied to him. But greater than all, the seeds of hatred sown through all his life now sprang up into flower.

The bitterness of old Alec, the tales he had heard in the woods and camps, the fights he himself had fought — all these things solidified the woodsman's spirit into hatred of McCurdy and his men. As for the old Mormon, that same hatred had been lying in his soul for twenty years; now in the fierce confidence of his fanaticism he saw an instrument placed ready to his hand.

"Listen!" he cried earnestly, leaning forward and gripping Jim's wrist. "Forget this petty scheme, friend! Why appeal to the law? Did McCurdy appeal to the law when he led his Gentiles upon us? Did Bedfort appeal to the law when he shot down the king from hiding? Did the law punish him for that deed? No! Your father dealt not with the Gentile law, either; he made laws for his people and ruled us after them. Nor should you stoop where he stooped not, James Strang!"

It was the first time ever Jim had been called by that name, which he knew now for his own by right. Alec had tried to tell him too late, but Alec would have told his other old friends, and confirmation would be easily obtained. But — was Alec to die unavenged?

"Listen!" went on the old man with increasing excitement, betraying a rather intimate knowledge of exterior things. "Why should you appeal to the law? Do you think it will avenge your friend's death upon McCurdy or his mate? It will not, James Strang! What care they for the law? They smuggle at will, wreck ships as we used to wreck them, conduct themselves far worse than ever we did under your father's rule. Did the law avenge us? Neither will it avenge you. They laugh at the law as we laughed at it — but in their pride, not in the faith. God was with us, James Strang, but He is not with them!"

"Huh! What do you mean?" inquired Jim moodily, feeling that the fierce vehemence of the old man was underlain by a stratum of truth. "Then why did the Mormon kingdom fail?"

"It did not fail!" and the quick answer was tinged with sadness. "Not until King James had been killed, until his people fell away from God even as the children of Nephi! The Lord chastened us for our iniquities, and sorely —"

At a groan from the other room he broke off abruptly, rose, and disappeared behind the tattered curtains. There came a low, fever-stricken wail of such heartfelt anguish that Jim thrilled to this cry of the mother desolate.

"My girl — my baby — see, one eye is blue and the other brown! Oh-h-h—" The wail died off into silence. Jim stared at the wall, and fell into tense doubtings of his own course. The old Mormon was right. Looking at it sanely, he felt convinced he could obtain no justice from Charlevoix. Gallegan would never be brought to book. King McCurdy was a power in the land, controlling the solid Beavers' vote; if need be, every man on the islands would swear that Gallegan had not gone to Mackinac on that cruise.

The woodsman stared at the chinked logs, his face grim as realization came over him. Who this old Mormon was he had not asked, nor did he care. He knew it would be useless to ask after his mother, yet when the other rejoined him he ventured the question. The old man tugged thoughtfully at his beard. "Your mother! No, I don't know her name — she died soon after your birth, I remember that. You were given to my uncle for fostering, I heard later you were lost —"

Jim nodded, frowning.

"Well, what am I to do?" he asked gloomily, "Unless I get the law after —"

The old man laughed — a harsh, terrible laugh Jim remembered for days to come.

"Who are you? Who are you? Is not James Strang's son heir to James Strang? Go and take your kingdom! It was not King James whom McCurdy despoiled, but you, his heir. It is not Gallegan whose life you seek, but McCurdy's, the man who protects the murderer!"

The primal instincts of the woodsman leaped into life. Without waiting to see the effect of his words, the old

Mormon turned to a rafter in the corner; and from above it took down a long, heavy rifle — an ancient enough weapon, yet one which had been excellent in its time.

"Look at this!" and he handed it to Jim.

The latter took it, weighed it in his hands, noted its fine condition and recent oiling. Flint was in the lock — and something more was upon the stock. Leaning over, Jim scanned the silver plate, to look up with a dancing flame in his eyes.

"James Jesse Strang!" he cried out, astounded. "Then — this was —"

"The king's rifle!"

The two men gazed each into the other's eyes for a long moment. The Mormon's face was grave, terrible, filled with stern light like the face of a judge bestowing a sentence which cannot be appealed. In the face of James Strang was a growing comprehension, a fierce flame of youth and ardent desire, an unspoken assent to what the other man had hinted. He was the dreamer, aroused to a greater dream than any he had yet known.

"Take it!" broke out the old man. "I give it to you for vengeance — king's blood for king's blood! Shoot the king as the king was shot, and take the kingdom of the disinherited if you can!"

Jim leaped to his feet, his green-gray eyes blazing. A new idea had come to him; an idea startling in its simplicity, in its greatness, in the sweep of wildfire it sent through his brain.

"I will do better!" and his voice leaped out in vibrant strength. "I will raid the island as McCurdy raided it — with my friends behind me! I will gather the French and breeds from Mackinac to Little Traverse, and my father's rifle shall speak for me and for you and the rest of those whom McCurdy scattered to the four winds!"

CHAPTER VI
HOW THE DREAMER DREAMED

"Then — you think it's a good plan, eh?"

"Ver' good," and Antoine Macfarlan nodded his huge, hairy head emphatically.

"Ah, you King McCurdy!" Marc Groscap leaped up excitedly, shaking his fist toward the sumac bushes in the creek. "You Tom Gallegan! We show you — by gar, we show you!"

James Strang laughed, and fell to wiping at the silver plate on his rifle.

Three weeks were nearly gone since he had met the old Mormon, and those three weeks had been big with destiny. Fired with his tremendous dream, Jim had gone direct to Camp Kegomic, twelve miles above Little Traverse on the creek. Here were gathered some twenty men under Antoine — a huge man who spoke seldom and reverenced Jim for the verse he made. This was almost the first of the timber camps, for most of the wood then gotten from the north country was "shipping wood" — hard, clear stuff which went to Chicago. The whole lake, shore from Traverse to Mackinaw was lined with docks, much tanbark also being shipped south.

Having heard Jim's story, Antoine and Marc at once confirmed the Mormon's words. Jim was the son of King Strang. Once the raid was done with it would count for a good deal, but just at present the two older men advised that it be kept secret. In the woods it mattered little who a man's parents had been; a man was taken at his own valuation, provided he backed it up. In Jim's case it would be different, for a huge ambition had been disclosed to the hot imaginations of the French and breeds.

First and foremost, the raid was not only pronounced feasible, but was entirely fitting and proper in the eyes of all. The story of the brutal killing of Alec Brosseau had spread far through the woods, as Alec had been known in every town and camp from Boyne to the straits. Naturally, the story Marc reported differed materially from the version of McCurdy's men; it was Marc's tale which had gone through the woods and stirred the remnant of the older generation to a frenzied madness. In this northwest corner of the peninsula the French were savagely at bay; the southern and eastern rivers were filled with log camps where the Irish ruled supreme, but through here there was still breathing space for the older race, who got out ties and posts and bark and shipping wood, and fought their enemies when they came to town. The tale of Alec's death had gone far through these scattered camps along the lake edge.

And with it had gone Marc and Jim. Immediately after reaching Camp Kegomic, the latter had broached his dream, and the whole camp, solidly French and Indian, had been roused into a wild flame of enthusiasm. Jim and Marc had set out, and had visited every French farm and timber camp in the county, and some outside the county. The work had taken a week and more; they had talked with men they could trust, and these had one and all agreed in high excitement.

The plan was simple and savage and brutal as had been the plan of those other raiders twenty years before. They would take ship at Little Traverse, where a schooner could be obtained easily enough. The woods leaders answered for sixty men in all, which should be ample. They would sail to Saint James between two days, land at dawn, and clear every Irish family from the island. The sweep would be complete. The island with its farms and timber would belong to whomever held it.

And why not? In this fashion had McCurdy and his men won it, and in this same fashion they would lose it. If the law were invoked, Jim himself would invoke the law to support his earlier rights to King Strang's heir-ship. Yet the law was not highly considered in the woods, and would hardly be brought into the matter. The whole thing was very simple.

The sight of King Strang's rifle had sent a flame of wildfire through the woods. There was no danger that any hint of the plot would be breathed, for only trusted men were taken into confidence, and a half dozen leaders were selected from the various camps or settlements with whom the final preparations would be agreed on. The ever-slumbering feud between French and Indian and Irish had been quickened by Alec's death into a savage demand for reprisal, and from Goodhart to Crooked Lake there blazed a vivid hatred against King McCurdy and his men — who stood forth in all eyes as representatives of the newer and stronger race who had conquered the lumber camps.

And brewing the pot of this vengeance was James Strang, who sat outside the bunkhouse at Camp Kegomic, lovingly polishing his father's rifle — and dreaming a great dream.

It was a rude place, this lumber camp, yet loved of Jim for its virile ruggedness, its hardy men, and sturdy life. Across the creek was a dense cedar swamp, while the camp itself stood in a clearing on higher ground. Close to the camp were a few shacks where lived half-breeds, and a little-used trail ran beside the creek to Little Traverse, whither the timber and cut ties or posts were rafted. For buildings there were only the large bunkhouse, the larger barn and tool shanty, and the chuck shack. The barn served as store with the blacksmith's shop added to one end; at the other end worked and lived Bert Latouche, who acted as storekeeper and clerk and scaler.

They were ten years old and more, and looked it, these camp buildings. They had been put up in the old days when first cuts were being made and timber was supposedly inexhaustible, and their balsam logs were still sound in solid thickness. The roofs alone were new, being formed of adzed boarding and tar paper; the chinks between the balsam logs had been stuffed with wedges, clay, and moss; the Windows were tiny and very dirty from smoke within and weather without.

Though not sanitary buildings, they went with the woods, and they were well enough for a small tie-and-post outfit like Antoine's, which was a timber camp and not a logging camp. Attached to the chuck shanty near the pump was the washhouse.

"Big storm tonight," observed Antoine, squinting up at the clouded sky. The men came piling from the chuck shack, having ended their noon meal, and he moved off to take charge of the work. Marc gave Jim a keen look from beneath his swarthy brows.

"Boy, what's de mattair wid you, huh? You got de fevair?"

"A touch of it," acknowledged Jim. "Nothing much, though. Any more news from Pete Lareau? This storm won't bust our meeting?"

"No worry, de storm don't mattair," and Marc tapped out his pipe as he rose. "No, dere's no news from Petit Traverse."

That evening was to take place the final meeting of the woods leaders, who were to assemble at Camp Kegomic and complete arrangements for the raid. Jim polished away somewhat listlessly. It was true that he had a touch of fever, and more than a touch, but he did not connect it with the sick woman in the cabin of the old Mormon.

For the past three weeks he had been laboring at an extreme tension, shored up day and night by the excitement of his great scheme, with no thought for his own well being. He had waded through swamp and muck and morass, climbed arbutus-blown hillsides, slept out beneath the stars, eaten when and where he found food. He had been driven onward by his one consuming thought, and had expended the splendid forces of his body in reckless profusion, ignorant that they were expending themselves on a more insidious struggle within him.

Now, however, he had been forced into cognizance of that struggle. Even his magnificent physique could not hold out forever, and during the previous night he had felt the first sweep of fever gripping him. The only medicine in camp was quinine and whisky, of which he had partaken freely; but he knew he was not himself by any means. He could not enjoy his pipe for one thing. His head felt light, and something indefinable was wrong with his whole bodily system. He had said nothing of it because this night was to see the final culmination of his planning, the fulfillment of his great newborn desire, and he dared not risk postponement. He must keep going at any cost.

A week before this had come news which had shown the need of a quick stroke at McCurdy's kingdom. Years earlier, there had been a mission on Beaver Island, but it had languished. After the passing of King Strang's hardworking settlers who had cleared the land in part, the island had fallen upon evil days. During this stagnancy the mission had not prospered.

In the end the Franciscan had died, and since that time there had been no mission. King McCurdy had discouraged it, and his people went to Charlevoix or Little Traverse when in need of spiritual comfort — which was seldom. At intervals a priest was sent over to the group of islands, but there were many people and scattered settlements through the North; since the old monastery at Arbre Croche had gone into decline it was hard to care for the spiritual children.

But now had come word that the mission was to be reestablished at Saint James, and that McCurdy himself had applied to Charlevoix for a missionary to be placed in permanent charge there. At this men had grinned widely. All knew how the king's daughter was come home again, and all guessed it was her hand that lay behind this new move, for McCurdy had always been satisfied to get along as he was. To the keener-minded this was also a sign that the old lawless order of things was breaking up in the Northland.

The Pete Lareau of whom Jim had spoken was their confidant at Little Traverse, and a few days previously word had passed up that he was ill, though the word was vague and perhaps untrue. If true, however, his illness might prove disconcerting to the plot, since Jim looked to Lareau to charter a schooner for the trip to Beaver Island. So it was with no little anxiety that he held down his growing fever by sheer will power, and waited for the night.

He tried hard to work that afternoon, first at the skidways, where the larger logs were piled, then with Marc at cutting out ties. But more than once the swart voyageur searched the younger face with anxious eyes, while Jim himself felt something amiss. His ax swung heavier than usual, and his strokes were anything but precise; when he came near to splitting his foot, he broke into a storm of savage cursing that betrayed how far from balanced he was. For Jim never swore, even in anger; he had been trained in the ways of the older generation.

"It's no use, Marc," he said at last, his head swimming. "The storm will break pretty soon anyhow. I don't feel quite right, for a fact. Guess I'll call it a day and go back to camp for some quinine."

"Not too much, boy," called Marc after him, and Jim nodded.

Upon reaching camp he sought out Bert Latouche and obtained some unmixed quinine, washing down the bitter dose with a wry face. Then he stretched out in his bunk and tried to concentrate his mind on what was to come that night, but without great success. An hour before supper the storm broke with a wild howl of wind from the west. Upon that the men came streaming back to camp, and almost at the same time the "delegates" began to come in in time for chuck. Jim roused himself to action.

There were little George St. Peter from Cross Village, red-shocked Jean Tache from Pellston side, gaunt Henri Gilbault from the northern camps near Levering, and others to the number of a half dozen. Some of them had tramped all day to reach here at the time appointed. Each and all of them arrived with a grim nod or a swift "B'jou!" and a hearty handshake to Jim. It was curious that while they greeted Macfarlan and the rest as equals, they looked at the bright-faced, eager Jim with odd deference.

It was no tribute to his physical powers; it was a silent acknowledgment that to him they looked for brains, leadership. They were dreamers one and all, uncouth children who could be swayed by no solid arguments, only by the magic of words, and long ere this had Jim's verses made subtle appeal to their quick imaginations.

There was no word of the great plot until after the meal was over and the rain-wet men were steaming out. There was gossip of camps and woods, however, and somewhat to his dismay Jim learned how the absent Pete Lareau was rumored to be very sick, having met with an accident the week before in shape of a billiard cue, during a drunken mêlée.

When the coffee was over at last, pipes were filled and the camp adjourned to the bunk-house through a lashing storm of rain, thunder crashing overhead, and lightning rending the heavens asunder. The preliminary awkwardness of the gathering was abruptly dispelled by lanky Henri Gilbault, who lit his pipe, swung up into a bunk, removed his wet shoes, and demanded that Jim read them a "chanson." The word was at once taken up with eagerness.

"Yes, Jim, a song!"

"Give us de chanson, Brosseau!"

"You make for read dat Jean le Longue chanson, Jim!"

The young woodsman, who had not eaten much supper and was feeling anything but well, finally assented. A few days before this he had written a verse which had pleased him hugely, nor did he make the mistake of holding it above the comprehension of his fellows. He had put himself into the verse, with the memory of Alec Brosseau's dead face as he had last seen it that terrible day at Mackinac, and he recited the lines from memory, with no hesitation or pose in the rendition.

"I've a new one, boys!" he smiled, cheeks flushed and eyes burning strangely. "I've called it the 'Wage of the Woods' — and I guess you'll know who it refers to."

One meaning look flashed around the faces under the smoky lamps, and he went on:

> "For work and ache and sweat, for toil and strife
> By spear and peavey, trap and saw and net,
> The wilderness gives men a wage of life —
> And sells it dear for toll of work and sweat.
>
> "Yet men gain something more — a grave apart
> Where the leaves whisper requiem to the stars;
> A dwelling close to God, an honest heart,
> Hands gnarled with toil and rough with honor's scars;
> Contempt from lesser men, perhaps; a strong,
> Sure faith in all the things that are not seen;
> A simple trust that Right is more than Wrong,
> Thanks unto God because the trees are green;
> And with it all, the sure respect of those
> Who labor at their side by wave or wood;
> The surety that He who made them knows
> How, while the ax may slip, it still is good!
>
> "So, for their labor and unceasing strife
> By ax and peavey, oar and saw and net,
> The wilderness gives greater wage than life —
> And sells it cheap, for toll of work and sweat!"

There was silence as he finished — the silence of men who understood, who had read into his words the half-sensed depths of their own souls and experience, and who felt that he had expressed the thing they could never express. This was the secret of James Strang's hold over these rough children — his expression of themselves, of their secret and repressed feelings. They knew well whose elegy that verse was, and how every line of it stood for the old comrade who had been murdered from among them.

As Jim glanced about him at the unkempt faces, he thrilled suddenly to his own power. He saw them with all their latent inborn poesy, their wistful heritage of imagination, brought out to the full. From the huge, moody-eyed Macfarlan, who plucked at his great beard and nodded to himself, down to the rat-faced little half-breed, St. Peter, who stared at the glowing stove with distended eyes, these men had passed silent judgment on his words and pronounced them good.

Jean Tache cleared his throat suddenly.

"Ah'm hear," he said slowly, "dat de good pries' she's made for put Alec in one ver' dam good grave at Mackinac,"

A nod of approbation passed around. The brown-frocked men who labored here in the semi-wilderness were loved; they were fishers of men, yet they used neither net nor spear, but only love. And with their love they bought love. These woods were not wild enough to breed skeptics, or civilized enough. Not until the timber was gone and the old breed of men was gone with it would smoother tongues reach into the Northland.

"Dis be de beeg storm," observed St. Peter after a space of silence. "I'm t'ink me it would be ver' good tarn for raid de Beavair, mebbeso."

The discussion was on.

"Well, we've got sixty men arranged for in all," said Jim, forcing his reeling head into coherence. "We can crowd aboard a schooner at Petit Traverse or at Cross Village, and reach the island in a few hours. Is there a craft at the village now, George?"

The other nodded.

"De *Anna J.*, she's come dis morning for take on tanbark an' wood, Jim."

"Good! She's large enough to carry us all. Shall we hire her for the trip or simply take her? We'd better do it at once, before she gets any deck load stowed."

There was a general stir as the men leaned forward. The critical moment had come; the die was about to be cast beyond recall, and Jim's tense eagerness began to be reflected in the swarthier faces lining bunks and walls. The thing had passed from dream into stern reality.

"Soon, den?" inquired Antoine sharply, with a keen look from beneath his bushy black brows.

Jim nodded. "Yes. I've got a touch of fever, boys, and it seems like it may get worse. If it does then you'll have to push her through regardless of me, because if this affair once drops it'll be apt to fall through altogether or be given away to some of McCurdy's friends."

There was a general nod of assent and anxiety, for all admitted the truth of his words. Already Jim was feeling more like himself, however. The excitement buoyed him up, his sense of mastery thrilled him, he felt himself indeed a king's son. His was the destiny to avenge the death of Alec — and beyond that the death of his father, of his father's friends, the destruction of his father's kingdom.

There would be a new kingdom on Beaver Island — this was the great, dominating thought surging within him. The looted farms would be taken over by these friends of his, the island would be theirs by right of might —

A wild blast of rain and wind howled down, and the door opened. Every eye went to it. Jim saw a figure standing there, a figure unknown to him. Not a word was spoken, yet the instant wave of suspicion and the vibrant gaze of the woodsmen's eyes was like a physical force sweeping over the assemblage.

For a moment the man stood there, looking at the startled group within. He was heavy set, covered by large rubber coat and dripping oilskin hat, but was plainly no woodsman. In the yellow lamplight Jim saw that his face was unbrowned, his hands long and white.

"Is this Camp Kegomic?" he asked in a rich and mellow voice.

"It is," answered Antoine, eying him with evident distaste and grudging the hospitality which could not be denied. "Come in and warm up."

The other entered and shut the door. Advancing to the stove, he glanced around sharply, seeming to sense the gleaming hostility of the eyes that were centered on him. Then he flung off hat and coat. Instantly a surge of new feeling swept every man there.

"I'm beg your pardon, père," cried Antoine hastily. With a leap he was out of his bunk and pressing the newcomer toward it. "Take my seat. Cookie! Get de bon père coffee an' grub! Marc, give me dem blanket!"

Groscap hastily passed him a pair of blankets. Antoine was already removing the dripping boots of the newcomer, and now he stripped off the rough socks and wrapped the chilled feet in the blankets. Behind him the others watched eagerly.

The man was plainly unknown to any there, but he wore the brown, hooded robe of a friar, girded with heavy beads and crucifix. Jim looked not at these, however; he was lost in contemplation of the face now fully revealed to his gaze.

At first glance it seemed ordinary, yet to the woodsman's eye it revealed strange depths which attracted him strongly and much against his will. The brow was high, the head nearly bald, while the nose stood out with the same masterful command as that of Jim himself. The nostrils were finely curved — a curve of compression and firm restraint which continued down to the strong mouth, but not too dominant chin. From under the uncurving, straight brows looked out deep brown eyes; they formed the most distinctive feature of the priest's features, by reason of their searching brilliancy and mastery. To Jim's notion they held a deep and disquieting purpose, though the feeling was indefinite; he had yet to learn that they could hold a pity as deep as their power, a sympathy as great as their strength.

Although the priest was evidently unknown to any of those present, no words passed until he had swallowed some coffee, refusing any food. Then Jim, with an irritated sense that the arrival had been most inopportune, leaned forward and became the spokesman. He felt the fever gripping him again in a swirling wave.

"How did you find your way up here, père? Were you lost in the storm?"

The brown eyes turned and clenched with his. Jim found a quiet, restrained humor in their depths which made him feel unaccountably belittled and at a loss.

"No, my son," and the other thanked Antoine for his care with a smiling nod, as the camp boss squatted on the floor, "I was not lost. I am named Valerius, and am a humble brother of the Order of St. Francis. I have been for two days in Little Traverse, detained on my road from Charlevoix to Cross Village."

This simple and straightforward announcement had a most disconcerting effect upon the gathered men. Jim caught the feeling and shared it. This priest was anything but welcome at their council. Every man there was fully cognizant of the fact that no word of the plot could be uttered before him, for firm character stood out in every line of that ruddy, well-nourished, powerful face. This man was no pale weakling to yield to their desires and leave the issue with God; instinctively had arisen the feeling that he was a stranger to their land who could not sympathize with their motives, yet they felt him as one not to be lightly flaunted. Therefore, they kept silence, and must keep silence until he was out of their way.

"You've tramped from Little Traverse?" queried Jim, the others only too glad to leave the talking to him. "Then you'll need rest. Antoine, better have Bert make up the bed in the storeroom with fresh blankets, so Père Valerius can get to sleep right away."

Before the camp boss could more than give a flicker of relief at this ingenious settlement of their difficulty, the priest raised a hand in protest. His eyes rested on Jim, and again the woodsman found a humor in the brown depths, as though his ruse had been pierced and understood fully.

"There is no hurry, my children — I am not tired, and the night is young. Also, I wish to know who you are. I hardly expected to find so many men *living* here!"

The slight trace of emphasis on the word suggested that the priest knew very well how the camp was swelled by its visitors. A suspicion swept into Jim's brain, only to vanish in absurdity, but the woodsmen glanced at each other uneasily. Antoine spoke up, however, introducing himself and the others. Jim, the last to be named, still gazed steadily at Père Valerius; his vague suspicion returned and added flame to the fever flame in his eyes, which now were green and luminous and narrowed. The priest smiled slightly.

"These men all belong to this camp?" he asked in the rich voice with its tones of fatherly interest which so captivated these rude children of the woods.

"Not all," returned Jim, steeling his will to battle with this dominant stranger. "Not all, père. We're having a meeting to discuss personal questions."

He made no effort to disguise his quiet hostility, and used the excellent English he had learned from Père Weikamp, for to the woodsmen he usually spoke in French or patois. The brown eyes rested on him for a long moment, then swept away.

"But you are all children of God? Perhaps I may prove of some assistance, if you will honor me with your trust. I am new to this country, yet men are alike wherever found, and I am here to help you."

There was an uneasy stir of feet, but Jim's gaze did not falter. He felt angered at the intrusion of this meddling priest at such a time. Also, the fever was hot within his brain and unsettled him somewhat.

"That is true, father," he replied quietly, battling with his unreasoning anger. "But let it wait until tomorrow. Our guests will remain for tonight, and there is plenty of time. You say yourself that you are a stranger in this country, so we would not venture to impose our woods problems and intricate questions upon you while you are so weary and in need of repose."

A quick glance of approbation gleamed from face to face. Jim, however, was suddenly startled. In the eyes of the priest he read a sternness, a swift frown; he knew instantly that he was taken for a man of higher caliber than the rest. Also, he found in the brown eyes a gleam of comprehension, of knowledge, which struck alarm into him.

"My children," and Père Valerius glanced at the tense faces with a rapid sweep of his eyes, imperious demand in his tone, "I told you that I was not lost, that I was seeking this camp. Come, trust me! What are these questions you have met to discuss?"

There was heavy silence, until Jim made answer, with anger raging in his brain:

"They are our affairs, not yours, Père Valerius."

The priest leaped out on the floor among them, his features springing into life.

"Not mine!" he exclaimed sternly, reprovingly. "Listen, my children! Last night a man named Pete Lareau died in my arms. Before he died he told me of this meeting, told me of its purpose, told me whom I would find here. It was for this that I came to you —"

"And what of it?" cried Jim hotly, all his fevered anger waking into a savage challenge. "What of it? What have we to do with you?"

"'What have I to do with thee?' " There was a quick softness in the priest's face, a compassion in his voice that lashed the woodsman bitterly. "I think, my son, that I have work to do in this camp tonight."

"Get to hell out of here!" shouted Jim in a wild rage, leaping up threateningly. There was an instant of astounded horror, then the bunk house was in confusion.

CHAPTER VII
AND QUARRELING WITH GOD
WENT FORTH EMPTY

"**P**eace, my children!"

The stern, piercing voice quieted the uproar instantly.

The men present were held in the grip of two tremendous emotions. They were filled with shocked horror at Jim's outburst; every instinct of their religious feeling, their reverence toward this man of God, was outraged by his mad words. Yet to a certain extent they were in a sudden terrible fear.

None knew what Pete Lareau might have babbled in his dying, or to whom. If their conspiracy were to become known, they would feel a swift vengeance. The situation sent a cold chill down the spine of every man there, and more than one of them were ready to support Jim in his raging defiance. Despite their reverence, they fell little short of hating Père Valerius in that instant.

As for Jim, he was at once regretful for his words, and showed it sullenly. With a desperate effort at forcing himself into, calmness, he succeeded to some extent, so that big Antoine released him from his wrapped arms; the others seated themselves in gloomy silence. Jim instinctively felt he was approaching a crisis, but he could not quell the fever that shook him relentlessly. Vaguely he felt he was adopting the wrong course; at the same time there was stark madness within him against this sternly poised man in the brown robe, who had stepped out of the storm and threatened to ruin all the great vision that was gleaming before his eyes.

"Peace, my children!" Père Valerius looked around, sensing instantly the conflict which filled the men about him. "Fear not — no man knows of this thing except myself. No man shall know of it from me, I promise you. Can you not trust me?"

He met uneasy glances, while Jim stared at him with somber eyes.

"We trus' you, Père Valerius," and Antoine struggled to voice his thought. "But dis business, it's not de religion." The words were weak. Marc Groscap leaned forward and spat into the stove with swift contempt.

"You better go back to de Traverse, Père Valerius," he said calmly.

"Dis boy Jim's got de fever. He's not know what he's say, but I'm tell you dis, Père Valerius; you better go back to de Petit Traverse."

There was a mutter of assent. The priest looked from face to face, and read only a sullen hostility. Jim glowered at him in open anger. With a swift motion, he reseated himself, wrapped the blankets about his feet once more, and smiled.

"Come, let us talk, my children," he said quietly, soothingly. "Why should you fear me, distrust me? I am one of you, no more. If you think that I come in anger and wrath, you are wrong, I come in love, I know of how Alec Brosseau was killed, and I know of your wrongs and the injustice you have met with. I am on my way to Beaver Island, where I go to lake up the service of God, and if you will trust me I may be able to help you."

So he was the new missionary, then! The men were startled; Jim fell new anger stirring within him. But the hostility of the others was abruptly slaked by that bit of information, and they were momentarily diverted

"How you come to de Traverse den?" queried the red-thatched Jean Tache, with some interest. "Why you don't go by de boat from Charlevoix?"

"I was already at Petoskey when the call came," answered the priest simply. "I was to go to Cross Village to visit some sick Indians, and there McCurdy's schooner was to meet me, but I was detained at Little Traverse by the death of Lareau. I suppose the marriage will be postponed now."

"Huh?" grunted Jean Tache, looking up. "What marriage, Père Valerius?"

"Why, the marriage of McCurdy's daughter. Hadn't you heard of it?"

Jim was startled anew, unreasonably so. He remembered the face of the girl on the wharf at Mackinac, as he had remembered it for many a day and night since then

"Who is she to marry, Père Valerius?" he asked, almost before he thought.

"A man named Gallegan, I understand."

"Gallegan? The murderer?" Jim leaped to his feet again, his face in a flame of fury, his eyes binning even as his brain felt burning. "The curse of God on him! He'll never many that girl if I have to stamp the black heart out of him! I'll —"

Quite unexpectedly he found himself gripped by two brown-clad arms that seemed of rimmed steel. He had never seen such anger m a man's face as looked out at him from the priest's brown eyes; he was shaken terribly then flung like a child back into his bunk. Père Valerius stood looking at him, aroused at last.

"Be silent!" cried the priest, with such stern fierceness in his tone that Jim lay awed for the moment. "Blasphemer, be silent! Who are you to invoke the curse of God?"

"Who am I?" Jim struggled up weakly, his senses whirling from fever and shock. "I am James Strang, the son of King Strang! Beaver Island is my rightful heritage, and deny it if you can, you meddling Franciscan!"

Now indeed descended a silence, born of wonder and awe, astounded amazement and wild suspicion. The men stated blankly, only Marc and Antoine having known the secret; the priest bent his eyes on Jim with an incredulous frown; few believed the words until the universally respected Marc Groscap came to the rescue. Leaning forward, Marc again spat into the stove, laughed terribly, and spoke with a calm certitude which overbore all doubt:

"Dat's be true, père. Dis feller, he's be de son of de ol' king. Now, mebbe you listen to me, Père Valerius."

In his simple, quiet speech he told the story of Alec Brosseau and Jim, while the latter lay back in his bunk with closed eyes. All things were whirling around him, he felt very weak and sick; the faintness was but momentary, yet even Marc's words sounded as if from fat away He realized that he must be very sick indeed

He heard Marc telling frankly of their plans, but forbore to interrupt. Little by little the wave of nausea ebbed and left him calmer. Thankful for the respite, he lay quietly listening with little care for the outcome, yet with resentment gradually growing stronger He felt instinctively that Père Valerius was attempting to wreck his great vision, and hated the man with all his fevered brain.

Marc Groscap spoke very frankly, bluntly, and with calm impartiality as to the ethics of the raid, being a man who rarely committed himself. While he talked, Antoine Macfarlan sat frowning at his boots; in a corner crouched George St. Peter, bitter of eye, watching the priest with the same sullen hostility which was hovering over the others. From the bunks and seats poured out the steady fumes of clay pipes and "T. & B.," mingled with a heavy odor of sweating bodies, steaming clothes and boots, and unkempt bedding. Otherwise the place would not have seemed like home to these woodsmen.

Yet no sign did Père Valerius give of disgust or impatience. He listened gravely, his eyes fixed now on one man, now on another; he was gauging each of them — measuring the qualities to be feared or used, developed or silenced, while Marc was speaking. The mere fact that Groscap, hoary master of cunning as he was, had taken up the argument showed how this level-eyed priest had been accepted as a man among men, and not for his cloth only.

"Well, my children," said he at length, good-humored warmth in his tone and features, "it's a great plan, a fine plan, and there's some one among you who's got a wealth of brains for leadership!"

There was a general grunt of surprise, and Jim was so astonished that even he sat up, only to meet that same quiet humor in the brown eyes which had so uneased him before.

"What!" he cried, staring in blank bewilderment. "Do you mean it?"

"To be sure I do!" and the other laughed outright, eyes twinkling. "And will you be the king of Beaver Island, like your father before you?"

Jim looked squarely at him for a long moment. He saw what the other men did not see — that the priest was laughing at him, mocking him. Or was it a whisper of the fever voices which were rippling through his brain?

"Yes!" he exclaimed, with slow decision. "I will take my father's kingdom, Père Valerius — and I'll do it in spite of McCurdy or you or any other man alive!"

"Good!" roared out Antoine suddenly, and his cry was echoed by the rest.

"Well, well!" smiled the priest, when the deep murmur had died away. His eye settled on Marc, whose swarthy face was gleaming with excitement. "Now, Marc Groscap, let us resume our conversation. You are not a young man — in fact, you are a trifle older than I myself. You have spent your life in this north country, and you know it better than I. What, in your opinion, is the first thing a good woodsman should learn?"

Marc was obviously flattered.

"Well," he returned, with slow deliberation, "I'm tell you what I think, père. De good jack, he's mus' be strong — ver' strong. He's mus' be hard like nails. He's mus' got for fight like hell, mebbeso. But he's got for learn dis one t'ing firs' of all, père; he's got for learn dat dere's be a — a what you call — a *balance* in de woods. De w'isky be ver' good in de town, but not in de woods. De snowshoe be good in de winter, but not in de summer. De woods be de big t'ing, de man's be de small t'ing. De man mus' remember dis, all de time. You understand me, pPre?" The priest nodded, as Marc gazed up at him with wrinkled brows.

"I understand," he returned steadily, perfect comprehension in his deep, rich voice. As a matter of fact, old Marc had rather vaguely stumbled upon a tremendous truth. "You mean that a man must be well poised, must do nothing which would outrage the settled order of the woods. That is true, just as the scientist must not try to swing the earth off its axis, or bring summer in place of winter. Therefore, I take it, the best-poised woodsman makes the best lumberjack, eh? And that is why our friend Jim Strang, here, is one of the best of you — simply because of his splendid poise."

Père Valerius looked at Jim while a swift mutter of assent ran around the group. The young woodsman met his gaze steadily and coldly, his head perfectly clear for the moment; he was not at all deceived, and his resentment was increasing in proportion as the priest gained stronger grip over the woodsmen.

"Do you, too, understand what Marc Groscap means?" came the direct question.

"Yes," returned Jim shortly. "It is true."

"My son," and to his surprise he read sincerity in those piercing brown eyes, "you are a splendid man. You have brains, some education, talents, the power to win men's love. I have heard of you at Charlevoix, at Petoskey, from men you never saw and who have never seen you. With all this, is it possible that you have not seen what underlies this cherished project of yours?"

"Out with it!" snapped Jim, irritated afresh by his own helplessness. His fine eyes were bloodshot, his usually clear face was flushed; the fever was sweeping over him again, but he battled it hard. "What do you mean?"

He could not fathom those brown eyes, now asparkle with denunciation, now soft with tenderness; but he felt Père Valerius was speaking, not to him, but through him at the men around. He was being used as an instrument, and the perfect poise of the priest maddened him the more.

"Is it possible, my son, that you have not seen how this project of yours is violating the balance of things? Have you not seen how, by carrying out your raid on McCurdy, you would be outraging the settled order? I am not speaking of the law, understand; I mean only what Marc meant — the woods is the big thing, man is the small thing. Do you not see how —"

"No, I don't!" shot out Jim combatively, pressing down the burning that swept over him. "You're wrong. It was done before, McCurdy himself did it, robbed the Mormon settlers of their farms and everything else, drove them out and scattered them broadcast over the northern coasts. This raid of ours is nothing but retribution."

"Retribution is not in the hands of man, my son," came the quiet reply.

"It is, here in Michigan!" flashed back Jim hotly, his eyes blazing from green to gray and back again. "The gospel of peace won't work here, as you'll find. If a man is struck, he hits back harder; if he goes down, he gets the calks in his face. That's what goes in this country — and we aren't the worst at that. Go over to the logging camps and find what kind of gospel the river-hogs preach!"

Père Valerius nodded, as there came a murmur of approving grunts.

"I know, my son. So you think because McCurdy led the former raid, that you can do it again? Do you not see how it would cause an upheaval?"

"No more than his own raid did!" cried Jim. "We will take Beaver Island and throw the Irish out, that's all. It was done before, and it can be done again."

"Yes. It was done before, twenty years ago. I should not wonder if some of you men sitting here took part in that raid under McCurdy." It was a shrewd shot. Marc Groscap began to puff heavily at his pipe, and Antoine's eyes looked troubled. Abruptly the priest's face became stern.

"But look you here, James Strang. That was done years ago; the island settlers had not been there very long, and were not rooted into the ground. They had brought a strange religion into the wilderness, and the wilderness men resented it; there was more than one murder, robbery, evil deed, before, the raid finished it all."

"Don't you call the murder of Alec Brosseau an evil deed, then?" Jim demanded angrily. "The Irish have driven us from the lumber camps into the farther slashings; they have done their killings also, and they have marked up a big score against themselves."

"Perhaps they say the same thing about you," returned the other mildly. "I do not defend them, my son. I do not judge them or you. But look at this, now. They have been settled on their farms —"

"Stolen farms, you mean," broke in Jim savagely.

"If you like. They have been settled on their stolen farms for twenty years, and have acquired title by law. The country has changed since the old days, James Strang. It is lawless enough now, but not so bad as it was then. A new generation has grown up on that island; men and women have been born there and have died there, and the day of raiding had been put' away from the memories of men, because it was a black blot upon history and so is best forgotten. Marc Groscap, is that raid a memory of which you like to think in. your peaceful moments?"

At this sudden side attack, Marc sent one swift look of uneasiness at the speaker. He did not know how much this priest knew, but he was no coward.

"No, Père Valerius, it's not be de good memory," he returned simply.

The priest's eyes swung back to Jim searchingly, accusingly.

"And you, James Strang? Do you want to carry such a thing upon your memory all through your life — such a load upon your conscience? Ah, my son, think, well! Think of the poor people you would send from their homes to —"

"I was sent from my home in the same fashion," lashed out Jim thickly. He was all but blind with the tobacco smoke and the inner pain that coursed through him. His body seemed to be burning up, and his brain was a shriveled mass of heavy slag that weighed terribly upon his head.

"What excuse is that for sending others away? Wrong does not right wrong, my son; surely these woods themselves should have taught you that wrong is never greater than right, however more powerful it may seem!"

Those words struck on Jim's soul like whips, scourging him to remembrance of the verse he had read after supper. The others remembered it, too, as he saw in their faces. They were troubled, perplexed.

"I'm t'ink me you's be right," spoke up Jean Tache heavily, "Père Valerius, dere's be de ver' sick fam'ly by my camp. De man, she's make for die soon, I'm t'ink me. Mebbe you go dere wid me tomorrow?"

"Gladly, my son, if I can be of use. He is a Christian, I hope?"

"I'm not know, père. I'm t'ink me he's got de crucifix on de wall —"

Jim's hand touched the rifle — the rifle of his father, and he gripped it in blind desperation. Too well he saw that Jean Tache, who had been one of the most savage and bitter of the woods leaders, had quietly acknowledged the authority of the priest in those words, had tacitly abandoned the great plot. It was maddening!

"Oh, if you were a man like other men!" he cried out, staggering to his feet and shaking his fist and rifle together in the air. "You hide behind your cloak of religion, steal my friends from me — you snake!" He whirled swiftly on the startled men behind him, a desperate appeal in his face and voice.

"Marc, you'll not leave me? You, Antoine? You, Henri Gilbault? You who knew old Alec and loved him — you'll not —"

He paused, fevered madness choking his words away to a groan. For no answering eyes flashed to his. The woodsmen looked away, at the floor, at the walls, at the priest — anywhere but into his burning eyes.

"Jim, I'm not know," spoke up Marc uneasily. "I'm t'ink dat mebbe we bettair wait —"

"Damn you!" exploded the young woodsman — a wild burst of almost incoherent rage seizing him; rage against these false friends of his, against Père Valerius, against all the world. "Damn you! I trusted you, and now you play me false like this after you had promised to back me up!"

His voice rose to a frenzied scream. The others leaped up in alarm as he turned to the priest, but Jim only held out his rifle, stark madness in his face.

"And you, Père Valerius — to hell with you and your sneaking tongue! I'm going to kill McCurdy, hear that? I'm going to kill the king as the king was killed — king's blood for king's blood! Damn you all! To hell with the lot of you!"

Whirling, he planted his fist full in Marc Groscap's face, flung open the door, and vanished into the storm-lashed night, with the rifle of King Strang still clutched in his hand, a terrible sobbing cry upon his lips.

CHAPTER VIII
HOW THE PHILISTINES MOCKED A FOOL

"To marry — Gallegan! To marry — Gallegan!"

Those three words formed James Strang's only memory of the time that followed his abrupt exit from the bunkhouse at Camp Kegomic. Behind him, the men were out with lanterns and jug dips, searching him through the storm while Père Valerius and Marc Groscap headed them, but he did not know this.

His mental breakdown was terrible. In something over an hour, a wandering priest had smashed his whole vision into ruin, had cut him away from his friends and flung him lonely into the woods; combined with this was the racking fever that had struck his brain into the same burning madness which consumed his body. During the last of that scene he had been to all intents a man crazed. After he had left the camp, he was completely out of his head with sickness and despair.

One lesser contributing factor to this condition was the realization that Mary McCurdy was to marry the murderer of Alec. He had often thought of the girl, and, remembering how she had seemed to join in his plea for justice, he had written more than one ecstatic verse with her face in mind. Jim was a clean man; Alec had had several half-breed or squaw wives, but he had brought up the boy in a stern veneration for women.

After leaving Camp Kegomic, Jim headed away, absolutely blind; into the woods. The rain was beating down, the wind was howling in from over the lake, but he strode on half naked and bareheaded, heedless of lashing boughs and clinging thorns, still gripping the old flintlock rifle in his hand.

Then it was that his woods training told. Raving and muttering wildly, guided by no light of reason but only by sheer brute instinct, he headed for the one home he had ever known — the shack of Alec Brosseau. It was six miles distant, across a tangled wilderness of cedar swamp, second-growth timber, burned hills, and scattered Ojibwa farms. The one persistent idea which stuck in his head was that he was going to kill King McCurdy, but even this was wholly irrational.

Yet it remained with him. He wakened toward sunset of the next day to find himself obsessed by it. He was in the old shack again, though he gave little heed to this fact; the storm had broken and then switched around into a steady gale from the south.

Jim did not come to himself, though he did waken to some slight degree of sense and sanity. He knew only one thing — he was going to Beaver Island to kill the king. Of food he had no thought, or of clothes. He was still wet, splashed with swamp mire and shredded by thorns, and the fever was again upon him full force.

Careless of his awful bodily condition, he dragged himself from the cabin to the creek and slaked his burning thirst. Then he staggered back, found his rifle, and took down Alec's old powder horn from the wall. He finished loading the weapon, and promptly fell into blank unconsciousness.

Again he wakened, after two days of fevered tossing. He was weak, very weak, but his brain was still inflamed to madness with that one idea — he was the son of King Strang, and he was going to kill as the king had been killed, then take his father's kingdom.

In a corner he found Alec's half-emptied flask of quinine and whisky mixed, and drained it recklessly. For a space it was food and drink to his famished, fever-worn body, and nerved him to action. Being drunk, utterly mad, and obsessed with his one crazed intention, he caught up the loaded rifle and reeled out of the cabin to the creek. This he followed down to the shore of the lake, where Marc's canoe lay hidden;

The effects of the reeking liquor lasted long enough to set him upon the highway of destiny. He was weak, very weak; he could only stagger and crawl to the bushes, and, upon reaching the canoe that Marc had laid up, groped his blind way to the shore. Evening was just falling. His shadowed brain took no heed of this, nor of the southern gale that still scudded across the heavens and howled down over the lake.

After vain efforts, he turned over the canoe and dragged it to the beach, rising and falling repeatedly. He could scarce drag the light craft that a few days before he would have held up with one hand. He found the paddles and put them in after the rifle, shoved off with a drunken laugh, then leaped in and paddled from shore.

He did not need to paddle far. When weakness came upon him and horrible faintness, he slumped forward and lay quiet. The stiff south wind caught the high bow of the canoe and blew the craft out unaided; it was a three-fathom canoe and stoutly built for lake travel, so that after enough water had slopped in over the stern to adjust its balance, it swept along with the wind filling the high bow and holding it steady. Whether because of his undeniable drunkenness or because of his magnificent constitution, the fever in Jim's body had almost run its course. It ebbed slowly, until he fell into a troubled sleep. The canoe drifted on past Ile au Galee — "Skillagalee" Island.

Coincidently the storm was practically over. Toward dawn the stars shone out and the wind fell away, so that when the topsail schooner *Mary*, nominally of Green Bay, but actually of Saint James, pulled out of Cross Village on her way to Mackinac, she sighted the tossing canoe an hour after sunrise and ran down to investigate.

Tom Gallegan was in command, holding a master's license. He was in a bitter mood that morning. Père Valerius had failed to meet him at the village after three days of waiting, so now he intended running on up to the straits in order to meet certain agents and load up with certain goods for illicit traffic. What was more, he had lost both topmasts and a brand-new royal in the blow, and was in a "black anger" which would have done credit to King McCurdy himself.

What added most to his bitterness, however, was Leny. She had come aboard for the trip; flouting Gallegan openly, she had calmly taken up with the cook, who happened to have money. Gallegan, who had been promoting the matter of his marriage with Mary McCurdy, was not minded to have the crew bear tales of him back to the king, so he had perforce pressed his vain suit in secret.

He was not at all in love with Leny, but she disliked him, and it irked the iron mate sorely to be flouted. It was Leny, in fact, who first sighted Jim's canoe. She was standing on the quarterdeck; fine figure of a woman — broad of hip, deep of bosom, with a huge mass of fluffy brown hair crowning her girl's face. In a way, the face was beautiful, it was perfect in its firm, regular lines, marred only by a too-full mouth and long-lashed lids which almost hid her eyes from sight. She had character, did Leny, and held a tremendous fascination for men. Morals she had none, she was a handsome barbarian, susceptible to any woods hero who took her passing fancy.

Gallegan, at the helm himself, ran the schooner into the wind in lee of the canoe laid by and scrutinized Jim with a muttered curse. His first impulse was to sheer off and let the woodsman drift; a word from Leny caused him to look again.

"They's somethin' wrong, Tom. It's Jim Brosseau, an' he looks sick, eh?"

More than once had Jim and Leny met and the young woodsman had always a smile and a passing word for the woman of pleasure — but no more. She had heard from Gallegan's crew of the fight at Mackinac, and gazed at the canoe with keen interest, Jim's careless passings had left more than one memory in her mind of his strong, handsome face.

Watching, they saw Jim toss his arms as he lay, saw the ghastly haggardness of his unkempt face and body. Gallegan abruptly ordered two of his men to the back ropes beneath the striker, sheeted in the spanker, and headed up to the canoe as she drifted down with the rolling waves.

A white foam crest smashed her squarely into the schooner's bows. The men leaned over and caught Jim; the shattered canoe filled and drifted off as Gallegan threw off the helm. Ordering a man to his place, he strode forward and stood looking down at the moaning and muttering woodsman; then he kneeled, listening. Leny joined the group. After a moment Gallegan glanced up sharply.

"Boys, was they a gun in that canoe?"

"Sure, they was an old musket," said one of the men who had caught Jim. "We, hadn't no chance to get her, thought."

"Well — listen!" exclaimed the mate, staring down again. "Would ye listen to him!"

The men crowded around in silence, while the unconscious woodsman muttered and raved. Suddenly Gallegan leaped to his feet with a startled oath. He kicked Jim heavily in the side, and again Jim moaned and straightened out.

"It's a black lie!" roared the mate furiously. "Hey, Hanlon! Lay for-'ard here! Go take the helm, one o' you."

The helmsman came shuffling forward. He was an evil old man, bent with years of labor, who sucked at an empty clay pipe as he came. Gallegan addressed a few swift words to him, and he leaned over Jim, then gave a sharp cry.

"He's dead!"

"No, he ain't dead," sneered the mate. "Not yet. Go on, now — tell us if he's crazy or not. You ought to know, Hanlon!"

Old Hanlon shoved his battered hat back on his head, staring down. Jim lay very quiet now, arms outflung; his deep red-gold hair was matted; his face seemed horribly emaciated and graven with lines of suffering and the beard fringing his jaw gave him a new appearance. Since his visit to Mackinac with Alec he had not shaven, first from careless grief, and later because he had been too busy to bother. Also, it may be, because he remembered that picture of the bearded King Strang in the old Mormon's cabin. Not all of Jim's mad folly could be laid to fever.

"Divil take me!" Hanlon straightened up in blank wonder, his jaw fallen. " 'Tis a true word, Tom, if looks do be countin' for anythin'! Sure, I was clost by whin they did lay out the dead king. The lad here might be the double of him for looks, savin' the blood that was in his hair. Losh, losh — years an' years ago that was, an' me —"

"Well, this one'll have blood in his hair before I'm through wid him," broke in Gallegan coarsely. He drew back to kick the unconscious figure again, when Leny pushed him roughly away and stood over Jim anger in her veiled eyes.

"Git back!" she cried determinedly. "Ye ould boozer! The boy's sick an' needs care. No matter who he thinks he is — you lay yer dirty foot to him again and I'll give ye whatfer, see?"

A slow laughing sneer crept into Gallegan's hard face while the men around broke into a coarse humor. The mate started to speak, then checked himself; finally he turned and motioned.

"Two of you carry him for'ard. Let Leny 'tend to him if she wants."

He was promptly obeyed. Jim was lifted and carried away, Leny following. Then Gallegan turned with a wide grin on his high-boned, virile features, and spoke. One or two of the dozen men crossed themselves stealthily, but as he continued they all broke into a V great shout of laughter — laughter which held a brutal under note in its ring. The iron mate was in no hurry either to reach Mackinac or return home. Foreseeing future trouble and interference, he was savagely set against reestablishing the island mission and had made no effort to locate the vanished Père Valerius — who was at that particular moment consoling a dying lumberjack, in the camp of Jean Tache.

As to his marriage with Mary McCurdy, that was a different thing. He was quite determined on that, and the king was more than willing to set up Gallegan as son-in-law and heir. Mary had proven less willing. Since the scene at Mackinac she had given Gallegan few words, openly protesting that she would never marry a confessed murderer. The iron mate, however, had no doubt that in time he would overcome her dislike. So he was in no haste to find Père Valerius.

Therefore, with the last remnant of the gale blown out and the sea fallen completely, he anchored in a cove by the portage across "Wabble Shanks" Point, and. sent his men ashore. They were nondescript seamen, part lumberjack, fishermen, and a dozen other trades, as occasion required. By night they had felled and stripped two trees under Gallegan's orders, and next morning took aboard the two topmasts for finishing and fitting. The mate had no mind to run up a bill for ship's stores, and a dozen men can accomplish a good deal in a day's time. That night he pulled anchor and took his leisurely way for Mackinac Island, arriving before dawn of the next morning with his topmasts in place.

In that day there were two companies of infantry stationed at the fort, but the only bar against smuggling was the revenue cutter — a most uncertain quantity. The shore officers were something of a joke to King McCurdy's men. Few were the northern saloons who dealt in licensed spirits, and smuggling was a respectable occupation — more so, in fact, than running whisky to the Indians. The latter was a light labor by which many highly esteemed men have founded fortunes in no very remote times, but it was one thing at which King McCurdy balked.

All of which serves to explain why three large fish boats from the Canadian Sault warped in alongside the *Mary* as she lay at the wharf, and maintained a steady and open exchange of cargo. Before noon this was completed. Over the transferred stuff, now in the schooner's hold, was stored a layer of fish kegs; more were stowed on deck, and Gallegan's men were ready for their fun. Leny was already gone, having long ago departed for the fort clad in her finest. She had tired of her present lover, and in her quite unashamed fashion meant to annex a bit of Uncle Sam's money — and said so openly to the disconsolate cook.

Meantime, however, she had tended Jim, who lay ironed to a bulkhead in the forepeak. She had fetched him the cook's blankets with plenty of food and drink, caring tenderly for him. In this she was aided by the cook himself, a brawny Galway man who had only recently arrived in the Northland and was already at odds with Gallegan.

Jim had slept and eaten hugely; the fever had fallen away altogether, leaving him with only the wreck of his former splendid body, and in spirit he was no less broken. He was amazed at the deft tenderness of Leny, who hovered about him constantly; the hands of a white woman were new in his life. While entertaining no doubt as to her morals, he felt that that was something not concerning him at all, and his gratitude was entirely oblivious of the unremittent watchfulness and the absorbed interest which drew more than one coarse jest upon the girl from the crew.

Now, however, she was gone, and all that morning Jim lay in the dark, brooding. Both Leny and the cook had told him of his babblings when first taken aboard, and now that Gallegan knew his whole crazy intentions, he expected little mercy. He cared little, however; all the gay boyishness had been stricken out of him. He remembered dimly what had happened at Camp Kegomic, and even his fierce hatred for Père Valerius had passed into a despondent realization that the priest had been right.

Gallegan had not forgotten him, nonetheless. When the last of the work was done, dinner over, and the three fish boats were standing out for the straits, two men came down the forepeak and freed Jim. At their rough jests, he gained a swift inkling of what was to follow.

He cared not; if Gallegan meant to kill him, so much the better.

The iron mate had no such immediate intention. Jim rose weakly to the deck and was promptly dragged to the wharf in the blinding sunshine. When he was able to face the glare of light, he saw Gallegan standing with a sneer on his thin lips, his eyes cold and cruel and taunting. There was an odor of rank whisky in the warm, spring air.

"Hello, King Strang!" cried the mate, with a laugh. "Ye'd started out for your kingdom, eh? Met us just in time, ye did. Saved yourself the throuble o' ceremony. It's proud we are to see ye here, King Strang!"

Answering laughs swept the circle of men, gathered on wharf and rail. Jim gazed at them with dulled eyes. There were no town folk in sight, even the soldiers keeping away from the water front with exceeding great care; there was not even a fisherman on the dock, for every one not desirous of a free fight kept well away when McCurdy's. schooner came in.

From the after rail the cook was surveying the scene, but kept well apart from the crowd, helpless to aid. Jim saw old Hanlon standing to one side, an evil grin on his wrinkled features and a length of trailing ground pine in his hand. He was twining it with blackberry branches into a rounded shape that had no significance for the woodsman.

"Now, lads," went on Gallegan, with a hiccup, "if ye'll be settin' King Strang on his throne, divil bless him, we'll invest his gracious majesty wid the royal robes! Lend his majesty your arm, Jerry, or he'll be stumblin' over the royal footstool —"

"Salute the king, ye lousy scuts!" roared out a voice.

With a drunken yell of delight, the crowd fell on Jim. One man caught him by the handcuffs and pretended to lead him toward the big spile, beside which stood Hanlon. The others tripped him, lashed him, kicked him when he fell, and yelled the while like schoolboys tormenting a dog, Finally they got him to the spile and lifted him to the top of it, five feet above the wharf floor. With drunken jests, they lashed him in place; drawing down his ironed wrists between his knees and lashing them also, they fell back to leave him drawn over and gazing down upon them.

Jim made no resistance; he was too weak, and had no thought of battle. He had a terrible consciousness of having dreamed a wild dream and failed in making it reality; he saw now the madness of that projected raid, and steadfastly held his thoughts far from self and the yelling gang surrounding him.

He was terribly changed from the fresh-faced young woodsman who had visited the island with Alec a month before, changed both by his sufferings and by the beard which fringed his face in molten gold, curling a little with the curl of his long hair. Ghastly pale as he was, his sunken eyes blazed out keen and clear with a strange depth in them, a strange inner power which struck more than one of the drunken crowd to silence.

"All right, Hanlon!" cried Gallegan, after a long pull at a flask. "Let's be havin' the corynation! Git out them royal robes, you. Cookie, go git the royal salute ready for the firin'!"

A wave of drunken applause swept up as two of the crowd plucked old Hanlon to their shoulders. Vaguely Jim tried to smile. The effort was vain, yet it struck a haunting shadow of beauty into his face.

"Don't worry, cookie," he gasped, his words all but lost in the uproar surging around. "The whole gang's drunk —"

He ceased with a sudden groan. The men, roaring out with a swinging chantey in unison, had lifted Hanlon behind the spile; holding the wreath of mingled pine and blackberry thorn, the old man brought it down over Jim's head and jammed it home with a howl of maudlin glee.

"Whoop-ee! They's a crown for ye, King Strang!"

At the same instant another hand flung a big red mackinaw over Jim's tattered shirt. He gazed down at the liquor-crazed men who danced and whooped about him; blood was streaming over his face, but he said nothing. He was past caring. Gallegan turned to the schooner.

"Where's that stuff for the royal salute, cookie? Wake up, ye scum!"

Then it was that the unnamed cook rose to his one moment of greatness. With desperation in his eyes, he swung down to the wharf and faced Gallegan squarely.

"I'm done wid ye!" he cried, in a shrill Galway brogue. "I'm done wid ye an' yer dommed sacrilege, and it's a sorry man yell be whin yer sinses do come back to ye —"

Gallegan shot out his fist with a roar, and cookie went over backward. He scrambled to his feet and set off up the wharf at a run. The iron mate laughed a wild laugh and leaped to the deck above, reappearing quickly with a pail of slops from the galley.

"Salute the king!" he shouted, and passed down the pail.

With a deep yell which told how their passions were aroused, the men began pelting Jim with the refuse, taunting him with every vile word they could bring to mind; but still he sat quiet and unreplying, chin sunken on breast. Flasks passed around again, then at a mutter of talk a group turned to Gallegan.

"We'll, be goin' up for a thrifle o' brush," cried one. "It'll make an iligant bit av a fire, Tom, whin it's piled around the spile!"

"Go fer it!" yelled Gallegan, in mad delight. "It'll make him talk, anyhow!"

They went reeling away, six of them, half the crew. Where that drunken madness would have ended there is no saying, for the town knew that Gallegan's men were on the rampage, and there was none to watch or interfere, save from a discreet distance. The cook's one great moment had carried him far past the saloon, however. Barely had the half of Gallegan's crew vanished with drunken snatches of song than the figure of Leny appeared coming down at a fluttering run. Cookie had known where to go for help.

She panted straight down the wharf, hair flying as she ran, and wrath plain in her face. Gallegan and his remaining men were too drunk to notice such little things, however, and the mate staggered out to meet her with a hard laugh.

"Here she is! Come on, darlin' — salute the king! Here y'are!"

And he pressed an ancient egg upon her.

The girl, for she was little more, had heard the cook's panted words, and had glimpsed the limp figure on the spile. Her eyes blazing, she took the egg from Gallegan and smashed it fair between the mate's eyes, following it up with a blow.

"Damn ye!" and her voice rang like a steel whip. "How —"

The mate came reeling back at her with a curse, but she stopped him with a quick cry, pointing to the east.

"Look out, Tom! The east channel!"

Something in her tone caused Gallegan and his men to turn. There was a smudge of smoke on the horizon.

"It's the cutter!" cried the girl fiercely. "They told me she was comin', an' I meant to send ye word —"

"Jump, ye scum!"

Gallegan's voice fairly bit; drunk as he had been, the danger sobered him. If the revenue cutter searched them, as she was sure to do, the *Mary* was lost and they with her. She was already a suspected craft. Wiping the dripping egg from his face, and with complete forgetfulness of Leny's action, he roared at his men:

"Git them lines in! Jump to them halyards, you!"

"Hold on, Tom!" cried one anxiously. "Half of the byes are up-town —"

"By the poker, leave 'em there! Here, you —" and he whirled on the startled Leny. "Git aboard an' pull lines!" Turning, he sighted the slumped figure on the spile. "Hey, there! Cut that feller loose an' sling him aboard. We'll be needin' every pair o' hands we got. Jump fast, you!"

Old Hanlon whipped out his knife, and Leny sprang to his aid. Between them they cut Jim loose; the refuse-covered, bleeding figure fell unconscious into the girl's arms. Leny was quite as strong as any man there, and she aided Hanlon to lift Jim over the rail and to the deck beyond. Dropping him, they leaped to obey the mate's frantic orders, for there was no time to find the vanished half crew.

A steady wind was coming down out of the east. As the three jibs, top, royal, and spanker, rose one by one, they caught and filled instantly. The jigger followed, and with that the lines were flung off. Five minutes later the schooner was heeling over until the water foamed along her lee scuppers, running toward the west channel like a frightened bird, while behind her the smudge of smoke had grown to a black dot.

As her brown canvas lessened, the figure of a brawny Galway man stood looking out after her, a deep yearning in his eyes. Whether he truly loved Leny or not — who can say? Unconsciously cookie had served his appointed part in the destiny of James Strang. Whether they be cooks or mail runners or Mormons, it takes many lesser men to fill the parts of destiny in a greater life. Yet, after all, who shall say if they be lesser men?

CHAPTER IX
AND WAKENED A MAN

Jim slid down the sharply inclined deck and fetched up in the lee scuppers with a rousing thump, while a rush of cold water flooded over him. At that juncture Gallegan eased off helm and sheets, the *Mary* stood directly west before the wind, the big booms swung out wing and wing, and she came to an even keel.

Wakened from his terrible coma, cleansed and refreshed and given new life by the swift foam of ice-cold water, Jim sat up. He found Leny at his side, and she pulled him to his feet, her veil-like lids hiding the frank pity in her eyes.

"What's happened?" he exclaimed in wonder, the events of the last few moments being an absolute blank to him.

Without answering, the girl turned and went to Gallegan, who had the wheel.

"Give me the key to them handcuffs, an' sharp about it!" she demanded, then cast a glance aloft. "Look out for yer topmast, ye dam' fool. Why don't ye get gear up in shipshape fashion? Where's that key?"

With one anxious look upward, Gallegan handed her the key, and she returned to Jim. In a few words she recounted what had happened.

"Cheer up," she concluded, "Tom's got his ax into ye, but you ain't on the skids yet, Jim. Buck up!"

The words shot like an electric jolt through Jim's brain. "You ain't on the skids yet!" The homely woods' parlance, referring to the stripped logs loaded on the andiron-like skids ready for rolling on wagon or into river, was singularly apt. Then, and through many a weary day thereafter, the phrase occurred to him and lent him new strength.

He felt as though wakened from a bad dream. His body was still weak, but somewhere within him a miracle had happened — a miracle of suffering and torture. He was sane, he had become a man, he saw all things differently. Clawing his way along the rail after a single low word of thanks to Leny, he came aft and joined Gallegan at the wheel.

The eyes of the two men met and clinched, those of Jim a green-shot, deeper gray than the hard steel of the mate's. The latter alone of the crew was completely sobered; he realized, as did Jim, that the hatred between them was grown too deep for word and blow; it was no longer a surface thing, but had become a quarrel to the death, a match of soul against soul.

So the eyes held gray on gray, while the clustered crew watched and waited. Then Gallegan's face flushed a little, he licked his lips, and his eyes flickered out to the horizon.

"Yell help work us to the Beavers for your freedom?" he asked thickly, not daring to refer to the scene they had just left. He knew of old that Jim was a good helmsman, and thoroughly distrusted his own half-sobered crew.

"Yes."

With the word, Jim accepted the proffered truce. There was a quiet steadiness in his bearing which drew a curious look from the other man.

"Then take the wheel. I've got to clear this mess o' tackle aloft. Steady as she goes."

"Steady as she goes," repeated Jim mechanically, and gripped the spokes as the mate went forward.

Gallegan's new topmasts had been hastily raised and the shrouds were set up in slovenly fashion, so that the gaff topsail was threatening to drag the new mizzen topmast out of her. Going at the men with fist and boot and voice, Gallegan literally flung them aloft and put things shipshape. When the stays and staysail stays were sent up, he bent on a topmast staysail and the added lift was at once apparent.

The *Mary* needed all the lift she could get, as might be seen with half an eye. She was heading straight west for Point Labarbe; the cutter, which Gallegan identified as the *Michigan,* had picked up their hasty departure and clearly meant to overhaul them, for she was not rounding into the harbor. Gallegan after another look through his battered glass, sent a roar to Jim.

"Strang! Bring her sou'west by south! Lay on them sheets an' braces, you!"

The schooner again lay over until her starboard rail was all but buried. The mate was determined not to send her cargo overboard until he was cornered, and was now running for Point McGulpin across the straits.

"Feel able to keep the trick till them boys sober up?" asked the mate, returning.

Jim nodded. "I'm all right," he said curtly. "What chance have we?"

"A bare one. She steams about a knot point four better'n we sail, with this breeze. We'll get a blow tonight likely. I'm goin' to head fer the Shanks, douse the lights, an' cut back into one o' them channels behind the huckleberry swamps, let her go by us, then light out for somewheres."

"Is weather coming on, then?"

"Glass droppin' like a bat out o' hell!" snapped the mate, and moved forward.

Jim eyed the binnacle with an ironic expression. It was a peculiar situation, this. By a twist of his arms he could wreak bitter vengeance by simply broaching to the schooner; with her press of sail caught flat aback, either the masts would go out of her or she would plump clown stern first.

Yet he was a man and no longer a boy — even Gallegan had realized that. If caught, Jim would go to prison with these men whom he hated, these men who had tortured and mocked him; if they got clear, his future was more indefinite. But he was not worried over the future. He had been crushed, and did not even blame Père Valerius for his crushing. He had become a man — the future would attend to itself.

The plan of the iron mate was simple. The afternoon was fast wasting, and they could keep clear of the cutter while daylight lasted. Along the shore to the south, between Mackinaw and Waugo-shance Point — the "Shanks" — was low and very swampy ground, with channels cutting through it here and there; the point beyond was long and narrow and was extended for several miles into the lake by shoals. The *Mary* could cut through one of the channels and lie hidden, while the steamer with her deeper draft would have to go on outside; provided the schooner could lie unperceived in the channel, the cutter would pass on and be tricked.

It would be no easy matter to run those channels in the dark, with a storm beating down, but Gallegan was fully equal to the task. Leny had taken charge of the galley and was cooking supper, and a little before sunset Gallegan relieved Jim at the wheel. The storm was now almost upon them. The sky was overcast in black masses with lightning streaking along the horizon, but the schooner was still a good two miles in the lead of the chase. Suddenly, the wind having long since switched around to the south, Jim and the others were aroused from their hasty meal in shelter of the forward house by a wild roar from Gallegan:

"Slack away on them yards! Clew up all! Git that stays'l in — lower away, ye lazy scum — clew up that royal an' top — hump yerselves or we're smashed!"

The men obeyed on the jump, and Jim plainly made out the smother of wind and rain sweeping up from the southwest which had alarmed the mate. Down fluttered the jigger, the upper canvas and outer jib were gathered in, while the jib, inner jib, and spanker were left out. It was a dangerous expedient, but it was now sink or swim — capture was no alternative. Jim stole one look at the grim, tight-clenched face of Gallegan, then the squall was upon them with a wild roar.

The schooner reeled and staggered far over; during one sickening instant Jim thought the weight of sail had dragged the masts out of her. Slowly she came up, however, as the big spanker freed itself. Gallegan whirled over the spokes, and they flew south again directly across the bows of the *Michigan,* two miles distant. Darkness was upon them, darkness and a fine, lashing rain which was lighted an instant later by a wild crackle of lightning. Gallegan ripped out a curse: "Douse them lights!"

The lamps, already lit and hung, were promptly doused, Jim drew close the hood of the binnacle, helping the mate at the wheel.

"We're safe if the lightning holds off!" he cried, and the other nodded.

With the wind risen to a swift gale, the rain ceased suddenly; the schooner was scudding for shelter like a storm-struck gull. Lightning played hard and fast along the lake horizon to the northwest, but not brilliantly enough to show their position; trusting that the schooner would stand it, Gallegan ordered the reefed jigger hoisted. With that, the *Mary* fairly lay on her starboard rail and foamed through the water. It was a mad and desperate effort to run clear of the steamer, and succeeded; Jim could catch the red port light of the *Michigan* behind them, then it vanished as they ran abreast of her.

"Fooled 'em, by crackey!" and Jim heard old Hanlon chuckling at his ear. "Fooled 'em, King Strang! Well go through thim swamps like the divil wint through Athlone, now!"

It was not to be, however. While they were still reaching for the coast, a blazing rip of lightning wrenched open the sky; drifting across the wind came a deep-toned whistle blast Gallegan fell to cursing furiously.

"They seen us! Now we got to double back with the start we got, double again, and try once more to git the swamps. In with that jigger! Help Jim here, Hanlon!"

The mate dashed forward, and Jim found himself looking over the helm spokes into the wrinkled face of the man who had tortured him that same afternoon. Hanlon caught the glance and grinned toothlessly.

"Bygones is bygones, lad!" he shouted, "and I'll be shakin' hands wid ye on it some day!"

Jim made no reply save a brief nod. It was hard for him to throw any strength on the bucking wheel, and he was glad when another man relieved him and he could stagger forward. Going to the deckhouse, he dropped into a bed and slept, while the schooner raced back Into the northeast. Having recovered the lead he had lost, Gallegan meant to run as long as he could, then double back once more to the swamps and try his trick anew.

When Jim wakened, he ran his hands over his body in the darkness, astonished. His ragged trousers and shirt had disappeared, though his moccasins were still on his feet; a fish-scented but sound pair of trousers and a flannel shirt had been put upon him while he slept, and a blanket flung over him. Who had done it, he never knew. He suspected Leny, but she later denied all knowledge of it. He concluded finally that it must have been one of the crew, obsessed with sober shame over that afternoon's work.

Stumbling out on deck. Jim went aft to feel the schooner resting on an even keel in still water. Close behind her was a line of ragged pine and swamp cedar; she lay forging slowly ahead, through one of the deep and narrow channels cutting the marshy ground. Jagged streaks of lightning were streaking the sky, and by the infrequent light Jim saw that between schooner and open lake was a few hundred yards of treeless shore swamp. She was safe from any lightning glare, lying against the background of trees with all sail furled save her royal.

A half mile offshore Jim caught the lights of the revenue cutter, green and white; the *Mary* had dodged into the channel unseen, by fine work on Gallegan's part, and the cutter was steaming back toward the straits in a vain pursuit.

"We've got 'em now!" cried the mate jubilantly, as the woodsman appeared. "We'll run through the channel, cut across the Shanks, and be gone before she can round the point!"

The men gathered in dark groups, watching the *Michigan's* light, while the schooner slowly but surely drifted ahead with her royal catching the wind from above the sheltering trees. To port lay the dank mass of swampland, black and more heartless than even the tossing whitecaps across the sandy marsh opposite.

"Well, it's over, byes!" cried a voice from the waist, as the green side light of the cutter vanished, leaving only her mast light visible. "We've fooled thim revnooers fine, we have that! Glory be, but —"

The voice was drowned in a terrific thunderbolt which struck the whole ship's deck into a picture upon Jim's brain. Intense blackness followed — then shrilled up one terrible cry of dismay, anger, and horror. Perhaps windblown from the swamp, a weird ball of ghastly fire was running from, the royal to the topsail yard!

Abruptly it swung off into the shrouds, then hopped back to the yard, rolled out to the end, and stuck fast Jim had often seen the phenomenon in the woods, yet even he was startled by the sight of it squatting there like a sentient thing. He never forgot the faces around him in that faint and ghostly light; Gallegan stood rooted to the deck, one man screamed out horribly, another fell to his knees in sobbing prayer. Others cursed or stood in paralyzed terror, watching.

"Mother o' God!" breathed the iron mate hoarsely. "It's a divil light — an' the damned corpse candle has give us away!"

Then Jim understood. Not the sight of the thing alone had smitten the mate with such swift dismay; it was a fear lest some hellish agency had betrayed them, and superstition had gripped the crew. Sitting there on the yard, the St. Elmo's light did not serve to throw the schooner into relief, but it did move at her own speed — a steady-glowing light which would at once be taken for a ship's lamp.

Their worst fears were realized when there came an abrupt blast of the cutter's whistle, and her side lights shone out as she swung around.

"We're gone!" and Gallegan sagged limply back against the taffrail. "She's seen us and knows we're pocketed!"

The others watched that baleful light in silence, broken only by the loud and frenzied praying of the man forward until another man shut him up with a blow. Jim seized the helm' just in time to swerve the schooner from a jutting snag of logs, and had a glimpse of Leny appearing from somewhere forward.

"Smash the thing!" he cried angrily. "Throw a pin at it, you fools!"

"Don't ye do it, b'ys!" shrieked a man from the darkness. " 'Tis the divil himself, or a ghost belike! L'ave the dommed thing be — 'tis what we git fer this day's doin's — l'ave the dommed corpse candle be!"

Angered at their rank fright, Jim whipped out a belaying pin and let fly. He missed the ghastly ball of radiance, but the pin struck the yard — and a most amazing thing ensued.

Jolted free from its perch, the glimmering light seemed to poise for a moment in full air. An eddy of wind caught it, and, sailing along in horrible silence, it passed back the length of the ship and slowly sailed away in the direction whence she had come, still maintaining its level height.

Slowly the ghastly light drifted along over the marsh, following the course of the channel, then it struck out to the lake. For a moment it held upon its level course, when, struck by the full force of the wind, it vanished with uncanny suddenness. The whole affair was exactly as if a ship had been feeling her way out of the channel, only to douse her light and run for Mackinaw.

"By the poker!" gasped the mate. "Look — look!"

Sure enough, the cutter had seen that light. She swung up into the wind once more, both sidelights showing; then her green starboard light alone was visible, as she headed back east along the coast to intercept the supposed vessel. There was another prolonged blast from her whistle.

"It's a howling miracle!" broke from Gallegan. "Give me them spokes — crack on sail, there! Jump, you!"

The men obeyed in lively fashion, but in silence. They were awed by the terrible and uncanny manner in which this demon of the storm had wrought their salvation out of disaster. More than one of them shrank from Jim as they worked. It was his hand which had dislodged the light, and men said a curse would follow him for the deed. Whereat Jim merely smiled and went about his business.

During the days that followed, he smiled more than once, in fact. By morning the storm was gone and the *Mary* with it — up Epoufette way along the northern shore, as the cutter was certain to make for Beaver Island on finding she had been tricked.

For three days they hung about the north shore, peddling tobacco and liquor as they went, then hauled about at Patterson and headed for home. And in the space of those days Jim discovered that many things had happened to him.

His parole was unswervingly accepted by Gallegan. Neither he nor the men mentioned the terrible and blasphemous thing they had clone at Mackinac; the men, in fact, were ashamed and showed it, but not so Gallegan. He had regained all his iron immobility and power; while he treated Jim exactly as one of his own men, the woodsman knew only too surely that between himself and the mate there was a deadly enmity, bound to leap out after the troublous winds were hushed.

Jim was fast winning back health; but he had changed, and could not quite gauge the nature of the change — though it was writ plainly enough in his face for others to read. He was not the same proud, youth-filled, capable man; his self-confidence was badly shattered, yet there was new poise in his deep eyes. His beard he retained from sheer carelessness.

The crew saw the change, more than one of them openly averting that the curse of the corpse candle was upon him. Gallegan, who could read men, knew well that it was no curse but something quite different. There was a new light in Jim's face which the male read for a danger mark in days to come. This was peculiar, because the light was one of fear.

Jim remembered the words of Père Valerius. It had come to him that his fevered madness, his utter wreckage, the terrible mockery of his crowning — all these had fallen upon him almost as one blow. Who, then, had dealt that blow?

His sufferings struck him back, back beyond Père Valerius, even beyond Alec; back to old Père Weikamp and earlier years. Jim had forgotten many things in his later days; religion and faith had become to him as things to, be gazed upon from afar. Now it was different.

Leny, acting as cook, and repulsing all advances from her admirers, was the only person on board whom Jim could trust. He talked much with her through these days, heedless of the half-veiled grins from the men. Her deep sympathy drew him, in an impersonal manner; in his quiet strength the girl found something new, and in his new gentleness she found a thing she had craved bitterly. Even his calm disregard of her sex was astonishing, for in it there was neither scorn nor contumely. Indeed, as Jim probed into her nature, he felt a deep sympathy and pity for this wastrel of the northern shores; beneath her unmoral impulse, beneath the driving of necessity which had cast her upon shame, he found surprising depths and blind gropings after higher things.

He was too occupied with himself, however, to spare much thought on Leny. He had been established in the eyes of all men as James Strang — and in bitterness, not after the fashion of which he had dreamed. It was not the brown-robed man with the piercing brown eyes who had broken him; it was not the mockery of Gallegan's crew which had bowed him; it was not the misery of absolute failure and humiliation which struck him into the dust. It was the Thing behind it all — or was it a Light?

This was the fear which lay within James Strang's saddened yet strengthened eyes. Not a weak fear, but that of one who has found himself; a fear above fear. He had been changed from a dreamer into one who faced realities. His poise was no longer self-assurance, but a sterner thing hard to name. All this change had not yet come to pass in completeness, but it was in the process; he was afraid.

He began to realize something of it when the *Mary* passed the lighthouse and headed into the empty harbor of Saint James, He stood beside Gallegan on the quarterdeck and gazed at the town and the sandy shores to the north, the high cliffs to the south. He looked at the great dune which had been named Mount Pisgah, he saw the long, wood-piled wharf where his father had been shot down by Bedfort, the beginnings of the king's highway stretching south to Gennesaret and the Jordan. As he gazed upon the kingdom which was not his, he thought of the mad dream he had dreamed — and a smile crept into his face.

Somewhere a wise man has written that the fear of God is the beginning of wisdom.

CHAPTER X
HOW THE KING'S SON CAME HOME

"**J**im!"

He turned, to gaze into the strange, half-veiled eyes of Leny. She put out a hand to his arm in frank appeal.

"What you goin' to do now? Got anywheres to go?"

"No," he smiled, wondering. "I'm — well, I'll have to let things work themselves out, 1 guess."

"Then come along wi' me, Jim," she said, flushing a little, but fighting down the hesitation which lay plain upon her. "I got a place down in the woods where you can lay up, an' I'll keep away —"

Her voice dropped as she searched his eyes. Jim hesitated, reading the honest sympathy stirring in the girl's heart, and shrank from telling her the brutal truth.

"Thanks, Leny," he said, at length, "but — I'd better not. I've got to see King McCurdy, and there's no telling what'll happen. I'll probably hit back for Cross Village in a hurry. You run along now, and never mind me."

She turned away from him with no more words.

As the schooner drew up to the wharf and her canvas fluttered down, a subtle change crept over the crew. They were home again, men and women were coming down to meet them, and they had returned in triumph. The ghostly light was forgotten, save as it had rescued them; the thing they had done at Mackinac was turned to a good joke, and they were once more the king's men.

"Where's the king?" cried Gallegan to the crowd on the wharf. The schooner slowly floated in, fenders out and linesmen ready with the ropes.

"Ain't seen him lately," came the answer from the wharf. "Heard he was down to the Jordan farm, workin'. Did ye fetch the priest?"

"No — ain't he come yet?" Gallegan stared in some surprise, but there was no further time for gossip. The lines whirled out, the bights were caught and flung over the spiles, and the crew snubbed the *Mary* into a peaceful rest.

Leny was the first ashore, and vanished amid a burst of laughter; but for the others there was work remaining. The bulk of the smuggled cargo had to be broken out, and townsmen appeared with wagons to receive it at the head of the wharf. The wagons wound off and were lost to sight on the highway; McCurdy's system was an excellent one. He was wont to boast that if any smuggled goods or wrecked loot came into Beaver Island it would never be found again. Which was quite true.

Jim gave a hand at the work, not at all certain of what lay before him. The crew were now in high spirits, and with their superstition forgotten they began to pile rude jests upon "King Strang." The story spread ashore swiftly enough, until those on the wharf also joined in the fun; Jim continued his work with lips clenched tight and a bitter ache in his heart.

He was in the hands of his foemen. He had come back to the land of his fathers only to be reviled thick and fast; there was no brutality, but these slow-spoken men whose tongues retained the faintest touch of Irish burr looked upon him as nothing short of a fool, saying so frankly.

When at length the crew began to stream off with the departing town folk, leaving the fish kegs piled neatly on the wharf, Jim drew a long breath of relief and sought the iron mate, who was changing into clean clothes in shelter of the after deck house. Even as he caught sight of Gallegan, a sudden thought flashed into his mind with optimistic cheer.

"You ain't on the skids yet!" It was as if he heard Leny's voice beside him, and the brave words came back to him, steadying him into coolness. No, he was not on the skids yet! He looked at the mate steadily.

"Well?" snapped Gallegan "Ain't you skipped out?"

"No. Am I free to go?"

"They ain't no one stoppin' ye McCurdy can find ye, all light, if you're wanted. When he hears 'bout ye, I'm thinkin' you'll be sent for quick enough!"

"Why so? Can't I leave the island?"

"Not without ye go on the *Mary*." Gallegan straightened up and looked at him. In his hard eyes of steel-gray there was a flame of venom. "Why, ye poor cussed fool! Before the king gets through with ye there won't be no more King Strang foolishness left to bother decent folks. He'll pound some sense into ye, understand? And if he don't, I will."

"So?" Jim eyed him with a flickering smile of irony. "And how about that scene at Mackinac? I suppose you'll be proud of it?"

"That? Oh, hell! Listen here, Strang. I was drunk then, but I ain't now. If —"

"And you were drunk the day you murdered old Alec, too."

Gallegan started, his fists clenching. But in Jim's face there was a new poise which held no outburst of temper, only a perfect mastery of self. Also, there was something else — something the iron mate could not understand, for he knew nothing of spiritual forces. He was a man of sheer facts, and recked naught of the keen spiritual strength he had brought out in this woodsman.

"Well, what about it?" he demanded menacingly.

"Nothing. You're a hard man, Gallegan. You've murdered and worse than murdered, and you're going to pay for it bitterly No — I don't mean that I'm going to make you pay. I've learned something in the past few weeks. Some day you and I will have a settling, but I don't know how it will come; what I do know is that you're going to be broken worse than you've ever broken any man in your time."

Gallegan stared hard at him, chest heaving. He did not understand. "Oh, is that so?" he sneered. "Well, put up your hands and start it, then!"

"I said that I am not concerned in it," and Jim smiled a little, "It's not a bodily breaking you're going to receive, Tom Gallegan. It's something worse. You'll be shown that you've got a soul — understand that? You're going to be broken inside, not outside. I was broken both ways, and I know it —"

He paused, trying to find words. He did not well understand his own thought and could not put it into speech easily, while the fact that Gallegan did not in the least comprehend his meaning halted him abruptly.

"Crazy as a loon!" muttered Gallegan. Then he took a step forward. "Now, Strang, you keep out o' my way, see? I don't love ye no more'n yon love me, but I don't aim to beat up no sick man. Git to hell out o' here, an' keep away from me or I'll murder ye — and I mean it. I'll do it if McCurdy don't, I'm goin' to run ye out o' this whole country, and if we hear any more o' them Kegomic jacks coming over here, there'll be a wholesale scatterin' of French an' breeds. Get me?"

Jim looked at him quietly, steadily fighting down the overmastering desire to plant his fist in that sneering, steel-eyed face. A month ago he would have crashed into Gallegan, even as he had done at Mackinac after Alec's death, with a fierce joy; now he stood quietly, with only the burning flame in his eyes denoting the struggle.

For a little Gallegan glared at him with hatred tingeing his high-boned features dull red. He tried to down the woodsman with the brutal power of his eyes as he had downed many a man ere this, but he failed. Jim was afraid of himself and not of Gallegan. He was unaware of the other's effort and simply looked deep into the man's eyes. Then those words recurred to him with fresh courage, "You ain't on the skids yet!" And at his faint smile Gallegan's lids went down.

"Git out o' here, before I murder ye!" muttered the mate thickly, and Jim turned.

It was late afternoon, and the sun was warm as he walked up the wharf toward the town beyond. By some odd trick of fate it was his first visit to the island. He had more than once worked on the *Mary*, but always from Cross Village to Mackinac and back; he had been up and down the shore fishing, but his work had never taken him out to the islands, and consequently it was all strange to him here.

Yet it was also strangely familiar. He had heard tales of this place by the hour. Only a short two weeks before, Marc had told him how Alec had found him the night of the raiding, and now Jim walked across to the old whipping post which still stood where it had been built — and used — by his father, King Strang, He sat down, mechanically filling his pipe. Over to one side was the desolate mission church, where had been the Temple of King Strang; the king's stockaded "castle" of rough-hewn logs still stood, and was now used as McCurdy's store. Jim looked out toward Mount Pisgah and the king's highway, recalling how it ran south through the half-cleared lands, past Lakes Galilee and Gennesaret, to the southern cliffs.

More than one of the townsmen saw him there — men who had fished with him and drunk with him in times past. Now they went on without a word, though many of them did not recognize him. Those who did, and who had heard his story from the schooner's crew, searched vainly for the old, light-hearted Jim Brosseau in the haggard-eyed, bearded man who sat under the whipping post with his golden hair aflame in the sunlight and his thin cheeks flushed slightly with his secret thoughts.

"There he is! There he is!"

Something cracked against the stout post, and a stone fell on Jim's shoulder. He roused himself at the childish shouts to see a half dozen ragged urchins gathered to one side, watching him half in fear and half in boldness. Even as he looked, they sent a shower of stones at him with a burst of taunting yells. One of the pebbles struck him on the cheek and drew blood.

He rose, and the group of children scattered, only to renew their attack from a distance. Jim looked at them, unmoving. He knew well they had heard their elders talking, and this was but the reflection of it. He was considered a madman, a fool — a poet. With a bitter laugh he glanced at the whipping post.

"They might tie me up here and give me a few lashes," he muttered. "It would be a fine touch of irony!"

Slowly he moved toward the highway which led away from the clustered group of houses, his moccasins raising a little cloud of dust.

"That's him! Give it to 'im, fellers! Hey, King Strang! King Strang!"

The boyish shouts followed him, but he did not heed them or the pattering stones that sang around him. He walked on, lost in abstraction of dulled bitterness; soon he had passed the last driftwood shanty. Then, with the town shut from sight, Pisgah behind him and the straight road before, he drew a deep breath and lifted his head.

"At least the trees are friends!" he said aloud, and strode on.

He did not know that already his story had run the length of the island.

Upon leaving Saint James behind, he flung off the depression which had been cast over him by the taunts and mockery of those children, and walked along the sandy highway with the beginnings of a song in his heart. After all, he was not on the skids yet! He had come back to real matter-of-fact by now; he knew he had been a fool and had paid dear for his folly, but all that lay behind him. He had learned his lesson, and now was bent on seeing this island of which he had heard so much.

Afterward he would get home in some fashion. That same night, perhaps, he could get hold of a boat or perhaps a canoe. Go back to Cross Village he would not. To him, "home" meant something beyond. He had alienated himself from the woodsmen, he felt. Either he might get to Mackinac and go on to the north, or else he could get to Charlevoix where he might ship on a lumber schooner or go into the southern logging camps. He had a swift vision of the great country of which he had heard — the cities and things of men lying somewhere in the far Southland.

"The past is dead!" he cried out, and it seemed to him that the spring of the woods echoed the thought back sweetly: "The past is dead — go forth into the world!"

He had not yet learned that all the world may be comprised in a few square miles of earth — and all the manner of men therein.

Now it is quite indisputable that man cannot live by bread alone, yet bread he must have. Even genius can only starve to a certain extent, and as the afternoon began to lengthen and the shadows of the trees to slant athwart the road, Jim remembered he had not eaten since morning, and was hungry. So upon sighting an uncouth farmhouse in a clearing with a few sparse, new-plowed acres behind it, he betook himself to the door and knocked, expecting only the usual free-and-easy hospitality of the woods.

He heard the sudden outcry of a peevish baby. The barred door was open to him by a sharp-faced woman of slatternly appearance. As Jim spoke, he had a glimpse of a battered ship's binnacle with board top taking the place of a table inside the room.

"If you have a bite to spare, I'd be glad to do any chores —"

"Oh — it's *you!*" broke out the woman with astonishing viciousness. "I've heard about you, Mormon's brat — now git!"

She reached forth, and Jim found the muzzle of a shotgun touching his chest. Without a word more he turned and walked away to the road.

The terrible despondency swept back upon him tenfold. He knew that all the island must have heard of him, then. There was no haven of peace for him. Wherever he went he would find only mockery and bitterness, hard words and harder hearts, black looks and caustic abuse. He was an outcast on every island.

A surge of savage hatred swept up within him, but he beat it back and stumbled onward. Gradually he cooled down and even began to hope. After all, this might have been an isolated case. Surely the rude hospitality of the woods could not be banished from this island, even for the son of King Strang!

"I'll try again," he decided, and passed his hand over his face. "And I guess I'll get rid of his beard, if I get a chance."

And so thinking, he came upon one of the older farms, in a cleared glade. Log house and frame barn nestled in front of a windbreak of tall pines, flowers bloomed out in reckless profusion, and there was the tinkle of cowbells on the sunset air. Walking in from the road, he saw a big, black-bearded man at work milking. At his approach the man looked up and eyed him sharply.

"Evening," said Jim abruptly, almost defiantly. "If you can —"

"You're young Strang, ain't ye?" broke in the other abruptly. Jim nodded. "Then wait a minute."

To Jim's surprise, the other rose, went to the barn, and disappeared. He returned at once with a long whip trailing behind him.

"Now," he said, with deliberate emphasis, planting himself two yards from Jim, "ye'll be the feller what the schooner brung down. They's many a tale gone round this day, me man. Ye started out for to murder King McCurdy, thinkin' ye'd take over the island after, eh? A good hiding will be doin' ye good, so here goes "

With which he drew back the whip, but Jim did not move. He looked at the man, waiting quietly, and making no effort to resist. The other looked into his gaunt face and paused abruptly. For a long moment he gazed into Jim's steady eyes; then, with a jerk, flung the whip toward the barn.

"Get out o' here before I kill ye!" he growled thickly.

Jim turned and went. He did not understand why this man had repeated Gallegan's very words. He did not realize why each of those men had found something in his face which had been beyond their comprehension — a spiritual strength and sureness which filled them with mingled fear and hatred. His quick temper had been crushed within him, both by his physical and mental sufferings.

Now, however, he was heartsick. He felt beyond a doubt what a pariah he was upon this island, and as the farm fell into the distance behind him he choked back sobs. He had cut off his friends and was cut off by his enemies. All that flashing vision of going forth into the world had faded abruptly, and he suffered all the terrible desolation of a boy. He cared nothing for the world, but he did care for this far corner of it — all the world he had ever known.

On and on he went, walking blindly and careless of his steps. Everything seemed closed before him, and he lost heart; what good to make a fresh start in a far country when he had failed so miserably here at home, where everything had been in his favor? Struggling with himself, he strode onward while the desolate despair clutched deeper at his heart. He was on the skids at last, he thought bitterly.

Stumbling, he fell forward into deep grass, not trying to save himself. For a long time he lay there, sobbing dry-eyed, in a wild surge of mixed emotions that left him bewildered and helpless. The sun was down beneath the trees, and the purple shadows had merged into the blue masses of twilight, when he raised his head with a choking cry.

"If I had only died there in the canoe —"

Startled out of himself, he broke off to stare at a man who sat upon a stump and looked at him. He had heard no one come, yet the man was there. An ugly man it was, with a shock of grizzled red hair, wide-set and watery-blue eyes, a coarse pug nose, and very thick lips — but the eyes were twinkling beyond a doubt.

"Sure," and the watcher spoke in a wheezy voice, chuckling, "and if ye'd died ye'd not be talkin' to ould Danny Basset, so it's a lucky man ye are the day!"

"Who — who the devil are you?" gasped Jim, and stared in blank amazement.

"Ah, would ye listen to him!" Danny Basset wheezed out another chuckle, his strong brogue more evident in the inflection of his voice than in his words themselves. "Sure, if ould Hanlon — bad luck to him! — hadn't brought up the whisky kegs this afternoon I might be puttin' the same question to you, James Strang!"

Jim sat up, blinking. The touch of humorous kindliness in the man's voice and eyes astonished him. Who was this Danny Basset?

"It's a sorry figure of a man ye are, James Strang," went on the old fellow coolly. "Now if ye had a bite an' a sup, an' a bit razor to be scrapin' your chin wid, there'd be more to ye."

"Man, who are you?" said Jim slowly, incredulous. "Do you know that I came here trying to kill McCurdy and take what had belonged to my father — that every hand on this island is set against me — that if you've the heart to be decent to me they'll make you suffer for it?"

"Not they," came the assured answer. "Sure, ould Danny is known far and wide, me lad! Well, well, I've heard the tale from ould Hanlon the day, me lad. What made ye do it?"

"I was a fool!" muttered Jim bitterly. The other emitted a wheezy chuckle.

"Thrue for ye, me lad! A fool ye've been, an' what man has not — will ye tell me that now? But ye'd be more of a fool if ye did not step along wid ould Danny. Come now, don't be bashful wid me, lad!"

Stooping swiftly, he caught Jim's hand and pulled him up, then turned and set out along a narrow path among the trees. Jim followed, hardly able to believe his own good fortune, and presently found the dark mass of a house looming among the trees ahead. Reaching it, he saw that it was a large frame building with a big barn at the rear. His guide threw open the door, led him inside, and pushed him into a chair while he lighted an oil lamp.

Ten minutes later Jim was sitting across a table in the farmhouse kitchen. His new friend seemed to be alone, but had no lack of provender; what was more, they ate from real china — a luxury Jim had seldom experienced — with silver utensils. When at length he leaned back with a sigh of deep content and drew forth his old pipe, Danny grinned and tossed him a plug of T.& B. "Ye worked hard to get it here, me lad, so ye'll keep it wid me compliments. Now ye look better, ye do that! Wait till I get shears an' me ould razor —"

Feeling as though he were living through a dream, Jim watched Danny return and pull up a chair. Then the shears began to snip in his beard, and the two sat in silence for ten minutes while Danny worked. At length he wiped away the last fleck of lather from Jim's face, folded his razor, and pushed back his chair. Taking another plug from his pocket, he began to whittle it into his hand, looking up occasionally.

"Ah, lad — 'tis a fine-lookin' man ould Danny has made of ye!" he announced with some pride. "Now, listen to me, James Strang, I like ye fine, I do that. I'd like to have ye on the place, belike. Now they's O'Neill, one o' thim lads what was left ashore at Mackinac, God help 'em whin McCurdy sees 'em ag'in! O'Neill was workin' on the place, he was, by now an' by then, clearin' land an' takin' out posts from the cedar back beyond. They's a shack down by the cliff, all iligant it is for a single man like yerself. Ye can come up here for yer chuck — it's only a matter of a mile or so down the shore from here. What say ye, me lad?'"

Jim looked at him.

"Do you mean it, Danny Basset?" he asked slowly. "If you do, I'll — yes, I'll take you up on it! I may not stay long, but I'll stay. And God bless —"

"Ah, now — none o' that," broke in Danny gruffly, scraping his feet on the floor. "Sure, think of the iligant talks we'll be havin' together!"

"But McCurdy will never stand for it," and Jim's face fell suddenly. "I'll have a show-down with Gallegan if I stay, too, and you'll only get into hot water —"

"Divil a fear o' that!" chuckled. Danny.

"Is this your farm, then?"

"No, no, lad! Now what would I be doin' wid a fine, grand place like this? No, 'tis the farm of me friend, which I do run for him when he's gone to one of his other places. And divil a bit will Gallegan touch finger to any one on the king's place!"

"Eh — what do you mean?" cried Jim quickly, starting up. "Is this —"

"Sure, who's else? Sit ye down, lad; sit ye down! 'Tis on King McCurdy's farm ye are, and what ould Danny Basset says not the king himself dare to say no to!"

Jim's face went white, and he was on his feet instantly with a sullen curse and a flood of furious protest. The old man rose swiftly and seized his arm, clinging to him with a wheezy cry.

"Now — now, me lad! Don't be makin' a fool of yersilf! Let me tell ye one thing, me lad!"

CHAPTER XI
AND WAS HUMBLED IN SPIRIT

"Ould Danny" had not lived sixty years for nothing. He had but one argument to fling at Jim, and to it Jim could make no answer for very shame.

"If ye're too proud to work beside ould Danny, git out! If ye pay for yer bread in sweat, what the divil do you care whose bread ye eat? 'Tis not charity, me lad!"

Jim cared a good deal whose bread he ate, but gave up. He consented to work for the man he had meant to kill, resolving to drink his bitter cup to the dregs. With the morning he stood in his little shack, gazing long at his face in the cracked glass; he hardly recognized it. The cheeks were sunken and the same thinness made the eyes seem deeper; yet he was astonished by the firmness of it all, accentuated by his gaunt aspect. Nose, mouth, chin, and jaw — he was certainly changed, and his new-felt inner strength and will power was reflected in the outer man.

To remain here required all his iron control. Danny had said that McCurdy would return shortly, and Jim knew he must soon meet the king. Forcing himself to it, to the huge satisfaction of Danny, he took up his ax and went forth to labor in his enemy's vineyard.

The farmhouse was a mile away down the shore, the shack being in a large patch of virgin timber extending to the farm itself, and traversed by a rude logging road. Almost equidistant between farm and shack was a sheer break in the limestone cliffs — a huge notch where some ancient cavern had crumpled, running far back and crossed by a rude timber bridge. Save for this it was impassable, and either side was thickly grown with trees and bush; also, the water half filled the notch, giving the effect of a miniature Norwegian fiord. The bridge and road ran some three hundred yards from the cliffs; the woods were traversed here and there by faint paths, but on either side the notch the timber formed a dense and seemingly impenetrable mass.

Such, then, was the setting in which he found himself placed after his wanderings. The shack was a tumbledown log cabin with a fish-shanty stove and a bunk, a cracked mirror and a pile of moldy Petoskey newspapers, and nothing else. The work around it — this was what Jim loved; the healthy, rugged ax work in the cedar-sweet spring, sun, with the rustle of waves from the nearby shore and the mainland blue on the horizon, twenty miles away.

During two days Jim labored in peace and thankfulness; with such farm food as he had never known before, and Danny Basset taking keen delight in his company. The old fellow had himself been on the famous raid, was possessed of a tremendous store of common sense, and was one of the few men whom McCurdy loved and respected. His homely philosophy fast restored Jim to balance, while the swing of ax and the smell of chipped cedar flung him back into his old healthy frame of mind.

Jim learned that the king's health had been failing of late. He had "lived his youth too hard," as Danny said. At such times he was wont to go into the woods with his ax as a curative, and just at present was building a shack on one of the clearings south of Lake Galilee. Danny also confirmed the fact that Gallegan had been chosen as a husband for Mary McCurdy, to become the king's heir; as for Père Valerius, he had not been heard from and might arrive any day.

With the third morning Jim was so far his former self that he put into verse a fragment of sturdy woods philosophy uttered by Danny at breakfast. "Don't be thinkin' about tomorry, me lad. Tomorry hangs on the day, mind that. Don't be rushin' afther a thing-let it come to you, like the pine trees, me lad. 'Tis an iligant song they do be singin', but only whin the wind takes the notion!"

So Jim worked, and hammered out his verse while he chopped, rude lines that swung with the ax. The more he grunted out the words, the better he liked them; when he had brought down his cedar he sat on it to rest and let his voice ring freely. It came to him how the verse was one Alec would have liked, and there was more than a touch of feeling in his clear voice while he pictured the old voyageur leaning on his ax and listening as he had done so often — and would do no more.

> We who have joyed in life's good,
> We who have laughed at despair,
> We who have sorrowed and stood side by side over our dead —
> Should we care
> For the things which will some day be said
> When we are sped? Truth is where —
> Where bestead?
>
> Here, for the life we shall live;
> Here, for the trust we shall find;
> Here, for the good we shall give

Careless of them that may come!
For the wind
Bloweth free, with no thought to the hum
Of the cedars behind! Faith is dumb,
And is blind!

For a moment he sat motionless, lost in fascination of the thing he had created. He knew not that he had voiced a cry older far than Danny Basset, nor would it have mattered to him. He had but caught a fragment of humble woods thought and had transposed it into newer phrasing; to him his verse breathed with Inspiration and left him a little awed. Its thought was hardly in accord with his own past actions, as Danny had doubtless known well; in fact, to Jim's mind, it was almost a self-denunciation.

"Who are you?"

The quiet, tense voice lifting from close behind him startled Jim from his musings. Who had overheard him, stealing upon him thus in the cedar thicket? What new stroke of humiliation was to follow so swiftly upon his poor exultation and shatter it?

He turned, and looked iInto the sea-blue eyes of Mary McCurdy.

"Oh — *you!*" She seemed to shrink back suddenly, no less startled than he.

Jim's pulses leaped to the sight of her — the firm, slender figure clad in flannel shirt and corduroy start, the strong, poised, beautiful face crowned by its mass of bronze-black hair, the life-filled eyes which held alarmed recognition in their depths. That she had seemed to shrink from him smote Jim with quick bitterness.

"Yes," he said quietly, "it is I — James Strang, the outcast. I thought I was alone here. Have you come to add another touch of mockery? You have a chance the others missed, since you overheard my chanson."

Before the words left him, he felt his mistake. His bitterness wounded her. He saw a light flash into her face which reminded him of the first deer he had ever shot years before. But she was McCurdy's daughter, and he steeled his heart.

"I — I did not come for that," she said, still gazing hard at him. "I did not know you were here —"

"Didn't Danny tell you?" he broke in with dry hostility. She must have come to the farm with her father that morning. "You're hardly on an aimless quest, I take it."

She flushed a little. The sea-blue eyes did not waver from his.

"No. Danny asked me to get his ax, which he had left here in the cabin —"

Then Jim understood the wiliness of "ould Danny," and felt an instant revulsion of spirit. He might have known that this level-eyed girl's heart held no mockery. At the thought, he smiled until the haunting beauty which was almost feminine leaped out in his strong face and transfigured it.

"I beg your pardon," he returned softly. "You see, I had rather lost faith in everyone — and it seems even Danny was up to his tricks!"

"Did you really make up that verse yourself?" she asked quickly.

"Danny and I made it," laughed Jim, and explained. Still watching his face as though fascinated by it, she sat down on the tree stump.

"We heard about you, and about what happened at Mackinac," she said simply. "Father is very angry — not at you, but at the men. Tell me, what are you doing here?"

Jim felt a wrench of fresh bitterness, and looked away from her beauty. At last he replied slowly, telling of his great dream; he glossed over nothing of his folly, but bore lightly on that mockery at Mackinac. At mention of Leny's name the girl flushed and nodded in understanding. Jim cursed himself inwardly for not having reflected that she might be unused to the frank woods ways and sensitive; after that he said no more of Leny.

What was he doing — here? That was hardest of all, for he could hardly explain even to himself, except by laying the kindly blame upon Danny's shoulders. He was humiliated, borne down by his own words, but when finally he had finished and brought his eyes back to her face he saw that she understood.

"Oh," she cried quickly, eagerly, "I am proud of Danny! And of you, too — if you were a poor, weak sort of man it would be different. But you're not, you're not! Now I know why you could write such lines as those — tell me, do you do things like that often?"

Almost before he knew it Jim found himself talking freely. He told her of his life on the mainland, of the books he had read, of the men he had known — but mostly of the last. He felt deep admiration for those men, even though he had alienated them.

"I'm sorry I hit Marc Groscap that night," he concluded. "He had been a true friend to me, but I was a fool and could not see it then. Now he and the rest will have washed their hands of me, and quite rightly."

"No — not if he's the kind of man you say," she rejoined slowly. "I think I can understand exactly why he and the others thought so much of you — but it's getting late and I'll have to go back home. Now I'm going to tell father a few things, and don't you worry about his attitude."

"I shan't," returned Jim dryly. "Nothing can touch me — now."

He watched her pass among the trees and disappear, then picked up his ax and fell to work with savage intensity. After a little he desisted; the morning was far gone and he was destined to meet McCurdy when he went in for lunch.

Quite naturally, Jim shrank from that meeting. He wanted to turn his back on Beaver Island and never show his face there again. Slowly the feeling died out before his stern self-command. As Danny had said, he must bow to the storm, suffer the humiliations, let the future shape itself as it surely would do. Resolutely he tried to accept his own dictum and to become even as the singing cedars waiting for the wind to waken them. It was hard, for he had found his greatest exultation in trying to bend fate to his will.

While he took his slow way through the cedar, over the bridge across the ravine, and on to the farm, Mary McCurdy's face returned to him and her words. With a thrill of warmth in his heart he realized that she did not share the universal hatred of him; in this girl and in old Danny he had found friends. She was like the women Père Weikamp had told him about — different from most of, those in the woods, and she appealed tremendously to him. He wondered if his unknown mother had been a woman like her.

At thought of Leny he smiled a little sadly. He felt sorry for Leny. He liked her very much; not that he would ever have idealized her, for he knew only too well what she was — but he accepted it with a thrill of pity for the girl herself. To his straightforward notion of things, she was a good woman irrespective of morals. This feeling, oddly enough, was not at all confined to Jim, but was general throughout the island. Leny Rath was in no sense a weak and dissolute woman, but commanded respect even from the woods wives who cursed her, and these were many enough.

Upon reaching the farmhouse, Jim found Mary helping Danny in the kitchen, while King McCurdy looked on. Whether Mary had spoken to her father or not, Jim could hardly determine, McCurdy gave him one keen look, a nod, and a greeting. It was a bitter moment for Jim, though made easy for him.

Beyond a doubt the king was looking badly. When they sat down to the meal — all eating together in the kitchen without formality — Jim noted the change in him. The powerful face and frame were thinned and shrunken, and the man's dominant will was all too evident; McCurdy was fighting disease as he had fought his other enemies, with every ounce of his massive energy to the fore.

Brought into close contact with him through the following days, Jim could not but admire this rude woodsman who had built himself into a veritable king. McCurdy said very little; when men came to him for justice he settled their disputes in a dozen words, and sent them away obedient to his slightest nod. With Jim, himself he never referred to the past, treating him exactly as he treated Danny. Each morning he came to the cedar thicket and joined in the work; Jim never knew of the quiet admiration his labor exacted from the other man, whose great fetish was efficiency.

Gallegan was absent, it appeared, having gone to Traverse City in the schooner with a load of tanbark. Meantime arrived a letter from Père Valerius. The priest had been detained at the camp of Jean Tache, but would go to Cross Village shortly and reach the island when he could. He might be expected at any time.

The evening after McCurdy's arrival, Danny Basset visited Jim's shack and spent a good two hours in quiet converse. He readily admitted having sent Mary to the spot, and gave Jim a twinkling glance.

"Ah, but she did give me the divil whin she was home!" he chuckled wheezily. "But whist, lad! I'll be tellin' ye somethin' now. She says to me: 'Danny, why didn't ye sind down to the Jordan whin first he come?' Do ye get the dhrift o' that, me lad?"

Chuckling again, he dug Jim in the ribs, but Jim changed the subject abruptly. Nonetheless, he remembered. She was not sorry for their meeting, then!

"Have ye met any one else around here?" asked Danny, when he rose to depart.

"Why, no! Who is there to meet?"

"Oh, nobody in particular, I was just wondhering to mesilf, lad. So long!"

Jim frowned over those words, but forgot them speedily. With the next afternoon he found that Mary was indeed not sorry for their meeting. She appeared where he was at work, and sat watching until he joined her on the fallen log and rested.

"Your father was not the man I expected to meet," said Jim slowly. "I had looked for a man like camp bosses I have known — bitter hard, hated by all round them, holding their authority by force of might. He's not that kind."

"No. He does a lot of good in little ways — I think they all love him," she replied, softness in her eyes and voice. "He's really finer than you would imagine — just, the opposite of Tom Gallegan. I think he used to be a hard man years ago; it was my mother's death changed him, I believe. Had you never seen him before?"

"Often, but always on the schooner or at work. Never at home like this,"

After which there was a bond between them. Each afternoon she came and joined Jim, sometimes watching, sometimes helping, sometimes sitting and talking. Jim found himself living in dream hours, listening and waiting for her coming; he saw no more of the farmhouse than the kitchen, nor wanted to. He found himself humbled before her, because, upon his unfolding the hidden things of his life, she understood.

He read her verses he had written, told her of the lumber camps on the mainland, of the men who worked in mill and fish boat, of their primitive yet wholesome ways of life and thought. To him they were like his own felled cedars — rough and splintered without, rugged and sturdy within. And because she was of the same northern stock, Mary McCurdy listened and understood.

With her, Jim fell out of the woods dialect he often used, and came back to the purer speech Père Weikamp had taught him. Once or twice he wondered if McCurdy knew of this growing intimacy, but cast off the thought with a shrug. As a matter of fact, the king was too busy to notice. There was difficulty over the tax reports, since he made a show of rendering the government its due, which was somewhat less than the government demanded.

On the fourth morning Jim went about his work as usual, expecting McCurdy to arrive at any moment. The king came not, and after a space Jim went down to the bridge spanning the ravine, in order to put up a new shoring where a timber had rotted away. And there he met with a distinct surprise. As he set foot upon the bridge, the bushes opposite were parted and Leny Rath came with a glad cry to meet him.

"Jim!" and her hands met his in a warm greeting that could not be denied. "I heard you was workin' for the king, but I didn't know ye was at the north slashin' or I'd 'a' come to see you. Ye look, fine, man!"

"Feeling good, Leny," laughed Jim easily, noting with a sudden wonder that she wore a cotton dress and was barefoot, as though working at a house near by. Yet there was no house nearer than McCurdy's. "How did you get here?"

She looked at him a moment with a curious smile. The sunlight struck full upon her strong, rather coarse features, and Jim idly noted that one of her eyes was blue, the other brown. Then her strangely veiling lids fell, as if to conceal the eyes.

"How'd I get here?" she repeated slowly, searching his face. "Why, Jim — I told ye I had a place down here, didn't I?"

"What d'you mean?" he asked in blank wonder. "You're not working at the farm —"

"Not yet," and she laughed harshly. "Sence the king's gal come, McCurdy's kep' me clost to home when I'm around here. Didn't ye know I had a shack over yonder?"

Jim followed her gesture, and found himself gazing at the dense thicket crowning the right of the notch, where the trees stretched back from the cliff to the bridge in a solid mass. He was astounded, for she was clearly speaking the truth.

"No, I didn't," he said slowly. "I don't see anything of a shack —"

"It ain't meant to be seen," came the reply. "The king give me the place last year, Jim — it's jest a little shack where I can be alone. Ye see, I was able to help him consid'able, once or twict, in foolin' the revnoo men —"

She turned in abrupt, startled silence. Jim looked up to see King McCurdy, ax in hand. McCurdy looked at them, his grim face set hard, then addressed the girl quietly:

"What'd I tell you about keepin' out o' sight, Leny?"

"I know — I jest seen Jim an' come out to speak to him," said the girl hurriedly, and departed with a smile. McCurdy watched her vanish in the bushes, then turned to Jim.

"Ye ain't mixin' up with her, Strang?"

"No," smiled Jim. "She was mighty good to me on that Mackinac cruise, though —"

"All right," McCurdy nodded curtly. "Long's ye know about her it ain't my affair. She's a good girl, but I can't have her around open like with Mary here. Ye see," and he took Jim's arm as they walked back to the cedar patch, "she's got brains, an' I feel kind o' sorry for her, so I give her a place of her own. She don't bring no men around her — every once in a while she takes a notion to be decent, an' holes up here. Funny, ain't it ?"

Openly Jim agreed; inwardly he thought it pathetic. He did not know that McCurdy had told the truth, but not the whole truth, about that shack of Leny's. He did, however, observe that the king had not taken his arm wholly from benevolence, for McCurdy leaned heavily on him and did little work all that morning. The old lion was sick, and already the carrion birds were gathering, though he knew it not.

CHAPTER XII
HOW KINGSHIP WAS DRIVEN FORTH

Jim saw no more of Leny that day, and with the next morning the king did not come to work at all. Therefore Jim abandoned ax work in the effort to get a verse fashioned by afternoon. He was carried away by Mary's visits and was blind to all else; the thought of being and talking with her was an intoxication such as he had never known. It lifted him to the heights, fired him with a wild flame of rapture; and, having finished his verse, he went to the farmhouse in a blind ecstasy — for it was a verse of love, and love was in him.

While dinner was forward, a horseman arrived with news which seemed to rouse the king from his moody silence. The schooner had been sighted beating up from the south; also, the revenue cutter was entering the harbor from the west. As the *Mary* had no illicit goods aboard, there was nothing of disquiet in the news save that the cutter had doubtless come to straighten out the tax tangle. Jim paid little heed, not guessing how those two vessels were even then bearing threads from the spindle of his fate.

Later, Mary McCurdy came and joined him as usual. Jim had waited all that day for her coming; now that she had arrived he felt sudden hesitation about reading his new verse. He had never known self-consciousness before, but her eyes were so kindly that he feared lest the direct meaning of his verse should banish that kindliness. Also, the return of Gallegan boded trouble. For a little the two sat silently, then Jim broached the subject nearest his thought.

"Is it true, Mary, that you're going to marry Tom Gallegan?" he asked bluntly.

She glanced away, her star-bright eyes clouded of a sudden.

"I — don't know, Jim. Father wants me to — but I can't do it. No, I'll *not* do it! I can't, after knowing that he's a murderer — anyway, I don't think I could bring myself to marry him. I hope father won't force me because — well, I'm afraid —"

She paused. Again silence fell between them, yet it was not oppressive. Man and woman as they were, they sat like two children in rapt listening. A robin had broken into song somewhere, and, as if provoked by the melody, a grosbeak closer at hand struck into a trilling flood of liquid notes.

Then the robin fell silent, with some abruptness, but Jim's wood-craft had deserted him. He was thinking of something else now.

"I wrote a verse this morning, Mary, for you."

"Good!" She settled back, watching his fine face, a laugh of sheer delight hiding in her eyes. "Read it. I love to hear your voice in the woods —"

Still hesitant, Jim spurred up his courage and obeyed, strength sweeping into his voice as the swing of the words sent his pulses leaping.

> "I will weave on a warp of God's beauty,
> A woof of the winds and stardust;
> I will fashion a fabric of duty
> And bind up its edges with trust;
> I will forge me a sword of decision
> And hilt it with faith sprung anew;
> And the world shall how down to my vision,
> For my vision is — you!
>
> "I will take of the tears of the gloaming.
> Of the delicate laughter of dawn,
> The splendor of sea surges foaming,
> The sweetness of days that are gone;
> I will fashion a song from my plunder,
> A song such as never man knew;
> And the world shall how down to my wonder.
> For my wonder is — you!
>
> "Till out on the lonely sand reaches
> And out on the desolate hills,
> And out on the palm-scattered beaches
> And out where the frost terror kills —
> Men shall hear my song ever reringing
> Till their heartache shall whisper them "True"!
> And the world shall bow down to my singing,
> For my song is of —"

Jim broke off suddenly, abruptly, even as the robin had broken off its song. Warned by some subtle sense, he turned and looked up into the grim face of King McCurdy. With a little intake of her breath the girl shrank away. The paper still clenched in his hand, Jim rose and met the sternly biting eyes.

"What's goin' on here?" demanded McCurdy acidly.

In a flash Jim knew why this man was feared. It was not for his mere physical power, great though that was, nor for his aggressive spirit. There was something deeper in King McCurdy — a force composed of many lesser forces, a strong elemental might which poised itself above the souls of lesser men like an eagle poising above a flock of gulls. As he stood gazing at Jim there was no particular menace in his attitude. Rather was it that of a man who sees himself defied by a child. His eyes were very cold.

"What's going on?" smiled Jim. "Nothing. Why?"

"Here's why, Jim Strang. I heard ye makin' love to the girl there. It won't do, I've took care of ye here, but now ye can git out."

Jim went deadly pale. McCurdy's whole attitude lashed him with its stinging contempt, but he fought down his anger.

"Why?" he parried weakly.

"Why! D'ye take me for a fool like yourself? D'ye think I don't know all about ye? Don't fool yourself. I've kept ye at work here to shame ye before the island — they're all laughin' at ye this minute. Fine king o' Beaver Island ye'd make!"

The scathing words reawakened all the old, desolation in Jim's heart. "I know I was a fool," he said slowly. "Yet you are a thief, McCurdy. You stole my father's kingdom — my kingdom. Everything you own was stolen property. You've wrecked ships here on the cliffs, you've murdered men and worse — yes, worse, for now you'd marry Mary to a drunken scoundrel —"

"That's enough!" broke in McCurdy thickly. His face had suddenly gone very white, which Jim took for a sign of anger. "Ye claim to be king, eh? Well, I *am* king. See?"

Jim looked at him steadily, unanswering. His very silence lashed the other man.

"Makin' love, were ye?" snapped the king fiercely. "After meetin' Leny right here yesterday mornin' an' makin' love to her, ye have the nerve to do the same by my —"

"You lie!" said Jim coldly. Mary's sudden movement was more than he could bear. "You lie, and know it!"

McCurdy's face went whiter yet. "Didn't I find ye talkin' to Leny on the bridge?" he demanded hoarsely.

"Yes," returned Jim hotly, "but you saw for yourself that I wasn't making love. Liar! Do you think you can set Mary against me that way?" He whirled swiftly on the girl, passionate appeal in his face, "Do you believe my word, Mary?"

She looked from one to the other, white-faced, frightened.

"Yes — I — don't ask me, Jim!" she broke out finally. "I know there's some mistake —"

"Mistake — hell!" lashed out McCurdy. "Git, ye Mormon! Hump yourself — git!"

His face was suddenly mottled. Jim glanced at Mary, but the girl was watching her father, hands at her breast. Silently Jim turned and departed, cutting through the woods toward the king's highway. He did not see the grim, erect figure behind him suddenly reel and clutch at a tree, nor did he hear the girl's swift cry.

In blind bitterness he reached the highway, crossed it, and flung himself down beneath a wild thorn apple just bursting into flower. There was no kindly Danny Basset to arouse him now; he lay silent and motionless until gradually the wild surge of emotion quieted within him, settling into a dull despair. How long he lay he did not know.

Again he had to cut himself off, but now he felt no sorrow, for he had not been a fool. He had read that in Mary McCurdy's eyes which set his pulses to leaping; he knew the king had read it also and feared him because of it. McCurdy had feared him! The thought was like wine to his head.

McCurdy should have good reason to fear him. The charge of making love to Leny was too ridiculous to be considered; he knew well that it could be dispelled with ease, even had Mary hesitated to believe his word as against that of her father. And McCurdy had feared him! Jim came to his feet, fired by a sudden new vision.

"The revenue cutter's in the harbor," he thought swiftly. "I can still get Gallegan jailed for Alec's murder, even if I can't get him convicted; then I'll sell the forty acres Alec left, buy in on a timber camp, get Mary whether the king agrees or not —"

He started north toward Saint James eagerly. Farm life and work had restored his sense of things practical, and now that the love dreaminess was torn away from him, Jim took up his plan and found it good. McCurdy should have good reason to fear —

Something like a giant bee sang overhead; the faint crack of a rifle followed quickly down the wind. Whirling, Jim saw half a dozen men running along the road toward him from the point where the highway branched off toward the king's farm. He heard their shrill yells, and guessed at once that McCurdy must have sent his men in chase. With a maddened rage settled upon him, Jim turned again toward the town and broke into a run; only to halt short as he saw Gallegan striding along the road. The mate had doubtless docked his schooner and was now seeking the king to make report. Behind him were coming two other figures, too distant for recognition.

Jim hesitated only a moment; then, driven into desperation and with a flame of hot anger striking through him, he went at Gallegan on the run. The iron mate saw both him and his pursuers, and stopped. The sight of that hard-lined face sent new hatred coursing through Jim's veins, and into all his splendid body leaped a savage desire to settle scores with Gallegan once and for all — while he still had the chance.

"They're hunting me like a mad dog," he half sobbed as he ran. "I'll show 'em I can bite — I've been humble long enough!"

The woodsman's intent was not far to see, and Gallegan read it at once. No words passed nor were any needed. Each man hated the other virulently, furiously. The mate had already heard that Jim was working at the farm, and had glimpsed behind the fact even more than the truth as regarded Mary; with jealousy adding fuel to his rage, he gave a single rasping curse and sprang to meet Jim.

The latter hurtled into him with blind anger, only to be met by a stinging blow which sent him sprawling in the sandy dust. Gallegan was after him instantly, and landed one savage kick; Jim managed to trip him up, gained his feet again, and the two men now came together with more caution.

For a space they stood toe to toe and slugged. Neither was scientific, and there were no rules to hinder. The mate, knowing better how to kill his man, struck hard for the body; Jim, seeking only vengeance, lashed out for the face. Gallegan was dealing with no whisky-sodden deck hand, however, and Jim took his punishment without wincing until at length he shot over his right to the jaw, and Gallegan was staggered.

Before he could recover Jim followed it up with a terrific right and left. The crushing blows went home. Gallegan reeled and flung himself into a desperate clinch, cursing and reaching up with his knee in a stomach punch, Jim, laughing a little, broke free and drove his fist into the hard jaw, and again. They were cruel blows. The mate lurched away, flung his arms wide, and collapsed into a crumpled heap.

Even as Jim followed, a stone crashed into his back. Turning with a snarl, he saw that during the brief encounter his pursuers had almost caught up. A shrill yell dinned into his ears:

"He's killed McCurdy. Git him, byes! He killed the king!"

Before the meaning of that yell quite penetrated Jim's consciousness, he heard the rifle crack again. Even as he turned to run, there came a stabbing flame through his right leg and he plunged forward into the dust. He struggled up, half mad with pain, found his leg unbroken, and tried to run. Another stone and another followed him; one struck his head and sent him down again blinded with blood.

He lay motionless, collecting his strength and waiting until they were upon him. He meant to get in one more blow at close quarters. A step thudded somewhere near by, and he gathered himself for a leap; then he was aware that the shouts had died into silence, that no more stones were falling. In what new role was fate now playing him as puppet?

"What means this, my children?" Jim quivered to the calm, sure voice which sounded above him. Incredulous, he lifted his head, slowly raised himself erect His head was swimming with pain, but he clearly recognized the face and figure of Père Valerius.

The priest was not regarding him, however. Standing a yard away, he was gazing at the little crowd of men who had stopped before his uplifted hand. Gallegan was just staggering to his feet, helped by two of them. At sight of Jim rising, they burst into a storm of wild invective and pressed forward. Père Valerius halted them with hand and voice and eye.

"Peace!" he cried sternly, and they fell silent. "You there with the rifle — come here and speak for the rest! What has this man done that you seek to murder him?"

The rifleman, one of the islanders whom Jim remembered to have seen among the crew of the schooner on that second trip to Mackinac, replied angrily.

"What's he done, is it? Why, he's killed the king, your riverince! McCurdy's gir-rl come fer us, tears all on the face av her, and we found the ould man sthruck down an' mutterin' av the felly here. So we come fer him, and what else would it be?"

"What's that you say?" Gallegan smote into the conversation, reeling forward unsteadily. The priest listened quietly while the man told Gallegan of how they had found McCurdy lying half senseless by Jim's shack. The mate uttered a savage oath, and turned to meet the brown eyes of the priest They struck him like a blow.

"To whom are you speaking, my son?"

"I — I — your pardon, father," muttered the mate thickly. "Who the divil are you?"

"Père Valerius, my son. Go and wash the blood from your face if you would speak with me."

The quiet words introduced an element almost of farce into a situation of tragedy. One or two of the men snickered. Gallegan flushed, then his jaw shot out angrily.

"I will not. Get away from that murderer!"

"You lie!" spoke up Jim, and his voice rang clear and hard. "You lie, all of you! I laid no hand on McCurdy. Go and ask his daughter, who was there."

He saw the priest look at him searchingly, curiously. Emboldened by the mate's defiant attitude, the men pressed forward, and Galle-gan took up the cudgels.

"If the king's sick," he growled blackly, "I'm in command here. You're not going to butt in and run things, understand? I'm master, not you. Get back to your mission and pray; that's what you're here for. Get away from that fellow!"

For all his threats, his gaze again fell before the stern brown eyes Jim, remembering the scene at Camp Kegomic, forgot his pain and waited for what he imagined would occur, though he was far from guessing what came. At the mate's words, Père Valerius drew him-self up a little. He stood very erect, his eyes going from face to face; in the warm afternoon sunshine his bald head shone white. The group listened intently for his words. Even his silence commanded them; when he spoke it was like a hammer blow.

"Until you come to me in repentance I pronounce you excommuni-cate."

In his voice was no hesitation, argument, room for appeal; only a cold finality. Jim saw the circle of faces go white. After an instant of astounded silence the man with the rifle took a step forward and fell to his knees with a cry.

"No — don't do it, your riverince! Sure, we'll be lettin' the lad go —"

Père Valerius raised a hand, and his eyes blazed forth.

"Begone to your homes! Blasphemers! I have heard what was done at Mackinac by you, Gallegan, and your men. Others have heard of it. Do you think such a thing is to pass unpunished? Go to your homes, and come to me at Saint James in repentance. Hypocrites, to think you can deceive me! Go!"

The men slunk away one by one, crushed by that imperious pro-nouncement. Of them all, Gallegan alone held his ground. He stared at the priest with all the strong passion of his nature aroused into activity, and now his gaze was not to be downed.

"Ye can cow dogs wid your religion," he said thickly, "but ye, can't cow men. Curse your impudence!" He cast a look over his shoulder, and flung a shout to his retreating men. "Hey! Come back here, ye fools!"

They paused, irresolute, not knowing what had happened. Before Gallegan could continue, the priest strode forward, and his steel fin-gers clamped down on the man's shoulders, so that the two stood face to face.

"Shame on you, my son!" said Père Valerius softly, yet Jim noted how the fingers sank into the mate's flesh. "Shame on you, who would revile those that seek to bring you light! I cow no one with *my* religion, as you term it falsely; it is not mine, my son, to turn to such purpose. Perhaps you already have another faith established here that you do not want me?"

"No," muttered Gallegan. He seemed fascinated, almost hypnotized, by those deep brown eyes. "None."

"Then do not decry any man, whatever his faith, who seeks to serve others," and with this he loosened his fingers, for a quiver of pain had shot athwart Gallegan's face, "Now go!"

The mate hesitated, then turned his back and strode off after the others.

So intensely had Jim been concentrated on this scene that he drew a deep sigh almost of relief as Gallegan departed. Père Valerius turned to him and put out his hands to Jim's shoulders, but his fingers rested lightly, and so deep was the sympathy and tenderness within the brown eyes that Jim could say no word.

"Ah, my son, you have suffered since we last met! Well, gray hairs will hurt no man if they reach not into the soul, Man, man, you have been fighting all the time? Is it meat and drink to you?"

At the whimsical note Jim smiled. He had no chance to reply, however, for now a new voice struck into his thoughts — new, yet old and dear.

"I'm t'ink dat Gallegan's one ver' sore feller now! B'jou, Jim!"

With a startled cry he twisted free of the priest to face Marc Groscap's extended hand and beaming face. His own hand went out.

"You — here!" he exclaimed, incredulous. "You bear me no ill will, Marc?"

"For dat crack on de jaw? Bah!" The old woodsman grinned in delight, "Mais non! What's make you look so queer, boy?"

"Nothing," and Jim flushed a little. Père Valerius smiled sadly.

"The scorn of men, Marc — the jeers and tauntings of men. Is it not so, my son?"

Jim looked from one to the other.

"I also am a man," he said slowly. "I owe you both amends and repentance, my friends. I wronged you at Camp Kegomic. How did you come here?"

"On the Michigan," explained the priest. "She stopped at Cross Village, and Lieutenant Bedfort brought us over. We had heard you were here, so Marc came in search of you, and I to take up my charge. It seems that I arrived barely in time," and he laughed. "What has happened here?"

Briefly Jim told his story, for the afternoon was waning. During the telling Marc got out his pipe and fell to smoking furiously, while the priest watched Jim's face keenly and searchingly; the tale of his humiliation was not an easy one.

"If McCurdy is really dying or sick," he concluded at a sudden thought, "his daughter is apt to have trouble with Gallegan, Père Valerius. She does not want to marry him. You will keep an eye on things, I hope?"

The other nodded thoughtfully.

"She shall be forced into nothing, my son. But who is this?"

Jim looked up to see Danny Basset trudging along the road toward them. At the same instant he became aware that his leg was bleeding painfully and he was weak. Marc caught him as he reeled, and lowered him to the road. The priest examined the wound, then fell to tearing at a handkerchief.

"A ragged flesh wound," he stated. "Not dangerous if you stay quiet, though,"

Danny strode up, doffing his battered hat to the priest as Jim introduced him.

"What's happened?" asked Père Valerius quickly. "Is McCurdy dead?" "Divil a bit — savin' your riverince," wheezed Danny. "'Tis a sick man he is, though. Thim fools did be thinkin' Jim had a hand in it, and off they whit. By the looks of 'em they found more'n they bargained for," and he grinned toward the clump of figures in the distance.

Upon questioning him, Père Valerius found that McCurdy had suffered a stroke of some sort and was really ill. He finished binding up Jim' leg, inquired the way to the farm, and then tucked up his robe.

"You two take care of Jim," he ordered briefly. "I must go where I am most needed. Farewell!"

He started off briskly along the road toward the farm. Jim, still sitting in the dust, looked up from one to the other of the old men.

"What's to be done?" he smiled. "Shall we go back to the farm or go aboard the cutter? Maybe we'd better make for the boat, Marc."

To his surprise Groscap dissented, while Danny nodded emphatically.

"Ye'd best do it, me lad, an' quick! I had a bit o' talk wid thim felleys his riverince sent packin'; Gallegan was sendin' off two o' thim byes to town by the woods paths, to be raisin the men on ye."

Danny went on to state that Gallegan, angered and embittered to the core, was determined to prevent Jim from reaching the refuge of the revenue cutter. As Danny had met the group, the mate was dispatching them to raise the scattered farmers and town folk. A certain proportion of the islanders would join the iron mate in defiance of the priest, and in case of McCurdy's death or sickness Gallegan was sure to be in absolute control of things.

"Why didn't you want me to go aboard the cutter, Marc?" asked Jim. "Danny could go on to town and send up a few men to protect us."

"Two reasons; boy," and Marc puffed sententiously at his pipe, seeming to be in no hurry whatever to get away, "Firs', who's be your fader? King Strang. An' who's kill de king, eh? Dat man Guillam Bedfort. Who's command dat cutter, eh ? De son of dat Guillam Bedfort. Mebbe you like for ask help from him? Well, anyhow, de secon' reason, Jim — dat cutter she's lef' de harbor by now. She's go clear for She-caw-go, I'm t'ink. me. Anyhow, she's be gone by now."

CHAPTER XIII
AND WENT INTO HIDING

Jim, equally with the other two, realized that his situation was anything but pleasant. Sunset was approaching, and within a short time he would be hunted far and wide, for Gallegan was practically in control of the island. The revenue cutter had only run in to land Père Valerius and Marc, load up with firewood, and be off to Chicago.

The tale of Jim's abortive plot was now common property. Marc, known as one of his friends and helpers, had been greeted by no half-veiled threats upon landing; the fact that he came on the revenue cutter reacted strongly against him. Only the company of Père Valerius had averted a row when Marc had started inquiries after Jim. Even had the *Michigan* remained in harbor, however, Jim could not have stomached the thought of appealing for aid to the son of his father's assassin.

Nor was he inclined to leave the island. The fight with Gallegan had fired his blood with a red flame of revolt, while the illness of the king left things hanging in the balance. Should McCurdy die Mary might eventually oust Gallegan by virtue of the king's lands and goods, which would to some extent establish her authority, but the mate would stop at nothing to get the reins into his hands.

"I don't know what to do, for a fact," frowned Jim, "Père Valerius could not protect us if we went to the farm, and Mary would be equally helpless against Gallegan's bunch. The king would not want to — and he stopped short. He was not minded to tell Marc the whole truth of that final scene with King McCurdy.

Danny extended his hand to Jim, clearing his throat noisily.

"Come — up wid ye, me lad!"

"Eh! What for?"

"Sure, if ye're betwixt the divil an' the deep sea, 'tis ould Danny Basset will have to be savin' ye. Into the woods wid the both of ye now, for I'm thinkin' men are comin' from town soon."

Jim rose, to find his leg stiff and extremely painful. Danny explained that there were short cuts through the woods to the town, and that Gallegan's messengers would soon have searchers out in all directions: Swift action was necessary, and he straightway outlined a plan while the three were seeking the shelter of the nearest trees.

"I hear ye met someone in the woods yestiddy," said Danny in a low voice. Jim started, then nodded, smiling. He knew now to what the old man had referred.

"Yes, I met Leny, and heard that she lived somewhere near. Why?"

"That's where we're goin'," returned Danny. "Listen now, the both of ye. I'm trustin' ye, Marc, so lay low wid what I'm tellin' ye."

Marc nodded gravely, and Danny proceeded to enlighten Jim on the subject of Leny and her peculiarly placed residence. It was quite true that King McCurdy had given her a home amid the thick woods, where no admirers were allowed, but it was quite as much from policy as from pity.

Leny's cabin was set back a hundred feet from the edge of the cliff. Directly below it was a cave whose mouth gave on the cliff shore; an opening in the rear led into Leny's cabin, which was built over the hole. In this cave King McCurdy was wont to conceal anything of especial value which was either smuggled or wrecked Aside from the king himself, only Danny, Gallegan, and old Hanlon knew of the place.

No little to his surprise Jim found that Leny in reality had spasmodic periods when she would make desperate efforts to live far from the garish lights. Then, despite McCurdy's kindly efforts, she would be gone to Charlevoix or Little Traverse or Petoskey, until she again returned in penitence.

"We'll stow ye in the cave," said Danny, "an' ye'll leave the island tonight."

His plan was simple and complete. Marc would ascertain the location of the notch in the cliff, then return to Saint James. That night it would be easy for him to take a canoe or fish boat from the harbor, slip down the coast, pick up Jim, and stand across for the mainland.

With no light heart Jim assented. He was not at all anxious to leave the island, but it would be impossible to long remain in hiding, since Gallegan would be sure to suspect Leny and search the cave sooner or later. When they had broken through the woods to the eastern shore, the two old men half carrying Jim, they caught sight of the *Michigan* a good mile offshore and standing south. Before her smoke had wisped out on the horizon the three were under the cliffs.

Indicating the position of the ravine to Marc, Danny here sent him back; the evening was upon them, and there was plenty of work in store for the old voyageur. When he arrived off the notch he was to flash a light, which Danny promised to be on watch for.

So Marc turned him about and was gone.

How he had got into the cave Jim had little idea. Gallegan's blows had hurt him more sorely than he had thought; his head was bleeding and rocking with pain from the stone blow; his right leg was throbbing and was almost useless. He knew that they were close to the half-flooded notch in the cliffs, and found himself climbing by Danny's aid. Then came blank darkness, and his face snuggled down to the cold rock in peace.

Danny saw that he had fainted, grunted in satisfaction, and pulled off his mackinaw to cover Jim's body, He then struck a match and vanished — not toward the cave mouth where they had entered, but along the steep slope in the cavern's rear.

A dream came to Jim — a dream of soft hands touching his brow, of old Alec, of an ancient schooner lying in Saint James harbor, of men who shot and thieved and laid the cloth for the feast of revolt to follow. In the midst of it all he wakened with old Alec's words still ringing in his head: "Ah'm put de stake in de sand for de dead man — hundaird of dem — de Mormon an' de voyageur —"

It was a gruesome dream, except for the soft hands, and Jim wakened to shiver in a soft gray light. He remembered now — he was in the cave beneath the cliffs. He lay nestled amid a pile of empty boxes, rubbish littering the stone floor around him.

"Bah goss!"' he muttered. "It must be day! Where's Marc?"

Trying to rise he collapsed with a groan; his leg was useless for the moment. He dragged, himself up, however, with set teeth. Twenty feet away was the cave mouth, a small, jagged opening through which showed the blue of sun-glinting water. It was broad daylight outside — and Marc had not come! The shock staggered him.

After a little he heard the scrape of feet and a murmur of voices, and gazed at the cave mouth to see two figures hastily enter. A cry of welcome broke from him at recognition of Danny and Mary McCurdy.

"Mary! What's happened ? Where's Marc, Danny?"

"No sayin', me lad, I was watchin' all night be he didn't come. Now I'll be smokin' me pipe outside, Mary, in case anyone do come by."

Whereupon Danny scrambled away, and disappeared. Then Jim forgot Marc and all things else, for Mary was kneeling beside him, her hands soft on his face — like those hands which had come in his dream, yet even softer.

"You poor boy!" she said, and when Jim reached up to catch at her hand, it gripped to his. He saw her face very grave and tender in the half-light, though it was pale and drawn. "Jim, father's very ill. Père Valerius thinks — thinks he's going to — to —"

"But — Mary, dear — you know I didn't hurt him?" pleaded Jim anxiously.

"Of course," and a wan light filled her eyes as they met his. "But

Gallegan won't listen to me, and he's raised the whole island against you."

"Then — you know I told the truth about — about Leny?"

"Yes," she answered quietly. "I could never believe that of you, Jim, unless I saw it myself. You — has she come down here?"

"No." With that Jim found that Danny had frankly told the girl the whole situation, including the little hidden shack above the cave. So he made no hesitation in telling of the unhappy girl's kindness to him on that Mackinac cruise; but, somewhat to his surprise, Mary received his words in cold silence. Knowing nothing of womankind, Jim proceeded to lay stress upon the kindly heart and strong character of the outcast — only to meet a gentle rebuff.

"But I wish you'd not be mixed up with her, Jim," said the girl softly. "It only does you harm, and it's not — not pleasant for your friends,"

Never having taken this view of the matter, Jim was blankly astonished.

"You'd not have me treat the poor girl as an outcast?" he asked earnestly. "Why, Mary — surely you wouldn't refuse throwing a ray of sunshine into her life? She's only a woman, after all, and you know how even your father feels a sort of respect for her —"

"Well, let's forget about her," and Mary laughed a little as her hands sought his bruised face once more. "You poor boy — how is your wounded leg?"

"Sore, but it'll be well enough," and Jim caught her hands fervently. "Look here, dear — will you go away with me — will you go away if I come back here for you after things have straightened out? Will you go back to the mainland with me, live in the woods, and —"

He paused, for her hands were trembling in his, and he found his voice suddenly choked and husky. He did not know how to say the thing surging up within him, but his arms went around her as she knelt, and drew her down closer to him, and the words broke forth impulsively:

"Mary, darling — I love you, Mary — I've never loved any one but you in all my life, and 1 want you! I need you —"

That was all. Before he quite realized what was happening, her face had come to his.

"Ah, my dear, my dear!" she cried softly as her fingers twined in his hair. "I trust you with all of me — I'll go anywhere with you, anywhere! I love you, Jim —"

He found her lips on his. They dwelt there in the dark, quiet, trembling, afraid of the thing which had come to them. They were but children, after all.

"I must go, dear —" and she pulled herself away suddenly, tremulously. "I forgot that farther is so ill — but I'll try and come back this afternoon or tonight. We may have news from your friend Groscap by then. Good-by, dear!"

"Good-by, and my heart to you!" added Jim softly. Her figure darkened the mouth of the cave, and she was gone.

For a space he lay infolded in a mighty exultation, then he remembered he had not eaten since the previous noon; so, falling upon the bundle of food Danny had fetched, he ate hugely. He still had pipe and plug, and when his hunger was satisfied he lay back and smoked, trying to realize the marvelous thing which had come to him.

But what was to follow? The situation seemed hard upon a crisis, if McCurdy were really dying. The king was passing, then, leaving a woman for his heritor; Gallegan was fast gathering the reins of control between his fingers, and Jim could see no present help for Mary McCurdy save in the doubtful strength of a priest. Whether spiritual strength could master actual power would be a new question in the north woods.

Once indeed it came to Jim that when McCurdy died the son of King Strang might rightfully claim the kingdom. He only smiled sadly. He knew how pitifully unreal was this moral right of his, how it would be mocked and laughed down in derision. No, he could not master fate; he must wait, wait for what was given to his hand.

Then in startling suddenness a new memory came to him — the memory of Leny's eyes as he had seen them there on the bridge over the ravine. "Where is my baby — see, one eye is blue, the other brown —" That pitiful wail of the mother disconsolate, which had followed him from the cabin of the old Mormon, now struck back into his mind. With a gasp he sat up, thinking hard. One of Leny's eyes was blue, the other brown! Never had Jim heard of such a thing as this; the swift thought that Leny might be the lost daughter of the old Mormon couple came to him with staggering force. Was it possible?

He lay there, lost in happiness and wonder, while the long day waxed and waned and the afternoon passed slowly. He could see nothing of the cavern behind him, save that the floor seemed to slope upward. Then, while the glimmer of blue water outside was fading away in the sunset glow, Leny came.

She arrived, not by way of the cave mouth, but with a glimmer of lantern light from behind. Jim caught sight of her figure and knew she must have come from the opening concealed by that hidden shack of hers. She sighted him, set down her lantern and a pail of water, and fell on her knees beside him.

"I met Danny this mornin' and he said ye was here," she cried softly, clenching his hand in cold fingers. "Ah, ye poor man! Them devils is out lookin' all over fer ye! Danny says to look after ye, so here goes. Lay still now."

Without heeding his protests, she firmly rolled him over and got at his wounded leg. With deft fingers she removed the bandage, washed out the ragged flesh tear, declared it to be healing well, and bound it up afresh. While she worked, Jim's mind was busied with the problem — had chance given him a clue which might yet serve to rescue her from this present life so pregnant with disaster?

"Tell me something, Leny," he said abruptly when she had finished her work. "Where'd you come from? Is your name really Leny Rath?"

In the yellow lantern light he saw a faint convulsion pass across her face, to be gone instantly. She dropped her head, and her fingers began to pluck at the mackinaw she had drawn over Jim's legs.

"I dunno," she returned slowly. "Ol' Fritz Rath, he brung me up down at Traverse City. He died when I was a kid, an' I went to work in the hotel dishwashin'. He allus used to say I wasn't no kin o' his'n, though. It ain't his picture in the locket, neither. Then I come to Charlevoix an' got a job waitin' table in the hotel, an' stayed there till — till I couldn't stand it no more."

"Locket?" asked Jim gravely. "What do you mean, Leny?"

She hesitated, then fumbled at her dress, and produced a small, cheap locket on its chain of brass, and held it down to the light. Jim raised himself on one elbow, laid his pipe aside, and opened the thing.

An old-fashioned tintype was disclosed — and at sight of the face he uttered a grunt of surprise. For beyond a doubt it was the face of the old Mormon who had given him his father's name and rifle. He stared at it, motionless.

"What's the matter, Jim?" inquired Leny, alarm in her voice. "It ain't no one ye know, is it? Fritz, he allus said he reckoned that feller was some kin to me —"

"Bah goss!" muttered Jim in slow wonder. A fear was upon him — was it his place to send back this poor wastrel to that sunken-eyed fanatic? Then he remembered the anguished cry of the sick woman, and knew that destiny had indeed laid a finger upon him.

Quietly, slowly, he told the girl who she was. He did not know the old Mormon's name, but he described the place, told of the sick woman calling for her lost baby, and mapped out the trail to the cabin.

Leny stared at him, first incredulous, then with slow belief dawning in her features. When he had finished, a great storm of emotion shook her; gripping his hands, she flung herself down with her head in his lap, sobbing unrestrainedly.

"Jim — I dassn't go there," she cried, a terrible desperation in her voice. "They'd throw me out — you know I ain't been good — everyone knows —"

Had it been a question of the stern old Mormon alone, Jim would have agreed with her at once. But again he told her of the sick woman.

"Don't look at it that way, Leny," he soothed her gently, a great pity for the girl consuming him. "There's nobody over there who knows you. The place is 'way off by itself in the woods, an' if you really want to make a new name for yourself, girl, go and do it."

She could not reply. Convulsive sobs shook her whole body, and the two sat in silence while gradually her emotion wore itself out. Jim held her to him, comforting her in awkward fashion, and suddenly a plan came to him.

"Have you heard anything of old Marc Groscap?" he asked quickly, explaining who Marc was, and his anxiety for the old man. She shook her head in mute denial, not raising herself.

"Well," continued Jim, "you go to Saint James and find him. He may be drunk, though I doubt it. If you can get hold of him, help him steal a boat and call for me here and I'll take you back home myself."

Her face came up — tear-wet and filled with such a splendor in the lantern light as never had Jim seen on woman's face before.

"Oh, Jim! Ye're so good to me — yes, I'll do it —"

There came a sudden interruption, as another voice broke in upon hers: "Oh — *you!*"

Jim looked up. Mary McCurdy was standing just outside the circle of light, and was watching them, her face smitten with anguish.

"What's the matter?" he cried hastily as Leny raised herself in quick alarm.

"Don't speak to me!" almost shrieked Mary, starting back. "Liar — oh, to think that you could go from me to — to *her!* Get away — don't touch me — and you talked of taking her home —"

Her voice rose to a furious cry as the amazed Leny would have stepped forward; then, turning abruptly, Mary vanished in the darkness.

Imploring her to remain, shouting after her desperately, Jim tried to follow. He stood up, struck his wounded leg against a box, and went down with a groan. He never knew what followed, for his brain was in a wild tumult of emotions. To think she could so misunderstand him!

He knew dimly that Leny tried to talk further, but only lay with his head on his arms, in bitter despair. Then he felt something brush his hail softly, and when coherence began to return, he looked up to find himself alone in the darkness, the lantern and Leny gone together.

It was a night of terrible agony which followed.

When at last Jim wakened from a troubled doze with a groan, he found that broad daylight sat outside the cave — it must be morning again. He heard Danny's wheeze, and found the old man sitting to one side, smoking.

"Danny!" he cried brokenly as his anguish came upon him afresh. "Did you see Mary —"

"Whist, lad!" Danny tossed a packet of food to him, which Jim left unheeded, "It was a dommed fool ye were —"

"But, listen!" In agony of impatience Jim poured forth his story, pleading with Danny to bring Mary back to explain the thing to her, to get Leny and make all things right again. When he had finished Danny spoke slowly:

"She'll not believe ye, me lad, though I do mesilf. She niver wants to be speakin' of ye ag'in, an' nigh bruk me head wid a plate whin I did try to set things right. The only way to be showin' her the mistake is to get Leny an' her together — which yell have a hard time doin' now, for Leny is gone — an' that divil Gallegan does be — runnin' things —"

Danny slowed down to a full stop. Something in his voice struck Jim with new fear.

"What's the matter, Danny?"

"The king's dead, me lad — God rist his sowl!"

That McCurdy was actually dead came as a distinct shock to Jim. He sat there in silence, not knowing what to say, sympathizing deeply with the old man who had known and loved McCurdy through so many years.

"He was a great man," said Jim at last very softly.

"Yis." Danny's pipe bowl glowed redly against the gloom. "An' he died well, he did that. He did not come to himsilf but for a minute, last night it was whin he died. An' in that minute, what did he do but be tellin' Gallegan the kingdom was his an' the girl wid it! He tould Mary to be takin' Gallegan, an' died. Divil an' all — why could he not have died contint?"

Between grief for McCurdy and anger at his dying words, old Danny was gripped in conflicting emotions. Jim stared into the darkness, and frowned; the iron hand of him showing even in death, King McCurdy had given a final grim twist to the situation by thus willing kingdom and daughter to Gallegan.

"Tis a big storm comin' up," observed Danny, with obvious effort.

"The last o' the spring gales, I'm thinkin'. The king'll be buried tomorry, me lad."

"Can't you get Leny to explain things to Mary?" asked Jim, reverting to his own troubles. "When is Marc coming? Tonight?"

"Ah — I'd been forgettin' Marc! No, me lad, he ain't comin' — not tonight nor no other night — ah, divil take that dommed Gallegan!" Danny roused himself to speak, and with wild anger and horror Jim heard him. Marc had reached Saint James as agreed, getting through the search parties by dint of his wily tongue. He had then gone about taking a fish boat and was beating out of the harbor without lights when an incoming craft ran him down. The fishermen promptly hauled Marc back to town as a boat thief, and threw him into irons on the schooner.

This news had come to the farm the previous afternoon; Mary had hurried down to tell Jim when she had found him with Leny. She had returned to the farm half distraught, to find her father dying. Gallegan waited until the king had passed, then set forth for Saint James; he and his men had hauled out Marc, tied him to the whipping post, and lashed him brutally while questioning him about Jim.

Old Marc had kept a tight mouth, being finally beaten into insensibility. At this juncture Leny had arrived on the scene. Somewhat frightened at their own work, Gallegan and his men incontinently bundled the half-dead voyageur into a boat, and two of the band had taken him off to be set ashore on the mainland. With them had gone Leny. By this time she and Marc had doubtless been landed and the boat was home again.

"They say history repeats itself," muttered Jim in a dull-bitterness of grief. "You know what caused the first raid, Danny? Only, the raiding will never come true again."

"Yis," wheezed the other, nodding, "Sure, I was at Arbre Croche whin the canoe thim Mormons set adrift did be comin' ashore. I mind me now o' Bennet an' his wife an' the little one — all wid their throats cut — ah, me lad, 'tis not good to be thinkin' about! 'Twas that same night we went aboard the *Able* an' sailed over —"

Danny was anything but pleasant company that evening. What with his reminiscences of King McCurdy, his rambling tales of Mormon days, and his detailed account of King Strang's famous treason trial at Detroit, Jim was heartily glad when at length his old friend rose.

"An' tomorry's the funeral," mumbled Danny, knocking out his pipe. "They's a big storm coming too. A grand wake they'll be, wid lashin's o' Canady West an' all hands dhrunk. Well, God rist ye, me lad!"

"So long," returned Jim helplessly, "I'll wait for what turns up."

And he fell into sleep again sobbing for the misery that lay upon him.

CHAPTER XIV
HOW THE KING'S SON
FELL AMONG THIEVES

All through that day and night Jim lay alone, brooding. With the dawn came Père Valerius, bringing him more food, but little comfort.

The priest had heard of Marc's brutal elimination from the scene, and found only uneasiness in the death of the king. There was storm in the sky and storm throughout the island. Exactly as had occurred at the death of King Strang, lawlessness again threatened to break out with the falling of the strong hand which had held it down.

Gallegan and one or two more were outlaws from the mainland. McCurdy had protected them and himself by solid control of the island votes, which ruled the county politics. The iron mate might do it also, but had none of the dead king's foresight and cold poise.

"I might excommunicate the whole island," sighed Père Valerius, discussing the situation with Jim, "but it would only end in my own failure. I've shot that bolt already. Only this morning Gallegan ordered two families deported — old enemies of his, it seems."

"But Mary — what of her?"

"She is helpless, my son — a chattel to go with her father's lands. Unless the revenue cutter returns to give us protection, nothing can be done."

Regarding Jim's terrible position in the girl's eyes, the priest could offer no consolation. Danny had told him all Mary, however, was broken with grief for her father, and stated baldly that she would listen to nothing about Jim. She neither believed Danny nor the priest, insisting she had seen and heard enough herself, and no faith could be put m Jim's lies. Even did Leny return, matters would be helped little, for Mary looked upon the story of the girl's parentage as a myth invented by Jim to excuse himself.

So Père Valerius departed, for the king was to be buried at Saint James that afternoon. It was like to be a stormy burial, with a wild gale blowing up from the southwest; as the storm was sure to last for a day or two, Jim could only bide in bitterness.

Blow after blow had fallen upon him. Each plan he made, great or small, seemed foredoomed to failure, while upon those who tried to help him he brought only sorrow and disaster. Even the king's death was due to him, though very indirectly. He wondered gloomily if the tide would never turn.

By noon there was a howling gale sweeping over the island and driving the clouds in a wild rack of gray scud. No rain had fallen, but the blackness to the south boded rain and to spare later.

With his leg healed enough to use, though painfully, Jim ensconced himself in the mouth of the cave and watched the tossing waters outside. He guessed it was still close to noon when he caught a sudden murmur of voices, and cautiously looked forth to see Tom Gallegan standing on the shore below, scrutinizing the path to the cave. With him were the old, evil-faced Hanlon and another man unknown to Jim.

"They's work for ye tonight," said Gallegan, his hard tones carrying easily to Jim, while his eyes swept cliff and shore. The face of old Hanlon contorted in a grimace of silent eagerness. "When the burial party gets to town, go out to the lighthouse an' slip the keeper some whisky. Plenty, mind; have him drunk by dark so they'll be no light the night."

Jim, listening, caught his breath quickly. Hanlon and the other man gave Gallegan one swift look of half-fearful admiration, then the old man chuckled:

"Faith, Tom, ye're runnin' things close —"

"Too good a chanct, an' prob'ly the last o' the spring gales," broke in the mate coldly. "String some men along the cliffs south o' town with beacons. We may catch a craft bound for Mackinac, and they'll be pickings. You," and he turned to the other man, "take care to the false beacon on the south point — the old place, ye know."

The hidden listener felt a surge of horror. Wreckings there had been before this, but only in the whispers of men. Until now the cold brutality of it had never been brought home to Jim in all its hard cruelty. And Gallegan was planning his deviltry for this very night!

It was cunning deviltry, too. The route to Mackinac lay between Beaver Island and Ile au Galee; by nightfall the gale would be a howling hurricane, and any trading schooner would be more than likely to strike into Saint James for shelter on her way north. With the light at the north side of the harbor gone, and a false light fixed on the south cliffs, the end would come with dread surety.

"Pass the word around," went on Gallegan, covering all points. "If anythin' comes ashore have the crowd ready to run to the beacon. We can use the fun'ral wagons."

Jim drew back from sight, staring blankly ahead of him, doubting his own hearing. The whole project was like some horrible phantasy which could not be true. An instant later his. thoughts were swiftly diverted to his own situation.

"An' if we do be gettin' the stuff," inquired the third man, "where'll it go? You mind how thim insurance men did raise the divil over that cargo o' flour the king hid away last year?"

Gallegan laughed, his harsh voice mingling with the evil chuckle of old Hanlon.

"Show him the cave, Hanlon. Best take a look around and see they's nothin' to interfere. If they's any boxes inside clear 'em out."

There was a clattering of stones as the two began the ascent.

Jim flung a rapid glance around. There was no place of concealment for him. White-faced, desperate, he backed away from the entrance, inwardly muttering a curse at his luck. Where was the rear entrance to Leny's abode he did not know. Hoping without hope, he drew back into the deeper shadow, and crouched there, waiting.

Hanlon's figure drew into the entrance, followed by that of the second man. A sulphur match flickered out. Jim looked around for a weapon, but could see none; the next instant a startled curse told him that he had been discovered.

"Gallegan!" Come up — the Mormon brat's here!" rang out Hanlon's voice.

In a desperate effort to get through them and break clear, Jim plunged forward and struck out. His fist drove into Hanlon and sent him reeling, but the other man grappled with him and brought him down, all three thrashing about the rock floor in mad combat.

Another match flashed up as the mate came rushing in. A glance showed him the situation, and with a yell he lunged forward. Jim felt himself dashed back against the rock; he tried to break free and rise, when Gallegan's fist caught him squarely on the chin and dropped him senseless.

With much loud and angry talking, the three men carried him outside and bound and gagged him fast. Then Gallegan dispatched Hanlon to the farm with all speed.

A terrific jolting slowly roused Jim from his unconsciousness. For a space he lay in a half stupor, only dimly awakened to himself. As the jolting continued, he became aware that he was bound hand and foot, and seemingly wrapped in dusty and dirty sacking. Gradually he placed himself.

He was lying in a wagon bottom, and the wagon was bumping slowly along a road. Men's feet rested upon him, and they were talking; one of the men was Hanlon, the other Gallegan himself. A rank breath of whisky came to him, and by the touch of accent to the mate's voice it seemed that the two were drinking. Also there was a dim sound of other wagons somewhere near, a thud of many hoofs and a hum of low voices.

"Look at his riverince beyand," jeered Gallegan, with a coarse laugh. "It's in his proper place he is, walkin' at the tail o' the king's hearse!"

Hanlon made an inaudible reply, but Jim stiffened out in his bonds, realizing now where he must be. Gallegan had evidently loaded him into a wagon, while he already knew that McCurdy's funeral procession was to go with the body to Saint James; therefore he must be somewhere in that procession, bound and helpless, given over utterly to his enemy!

To think of any escape was out of the question. He was absolutely beyond aid, and firmly tied up. Probably, he reasoned, Gallegan had kept his capture a strict secret.

"L'ave the bottle be!" commanded the mate abruptly. "Ye'll be needin' your head the night, Hanlon, and so'll I. Put it up, I say!"

Hanlon muttered again, but seemingly obeyed. While the jolting continued, Jim began to hear a shrill chorus of women's voices wailing from somewhere ahead.

"Hark to the women!" laughed Gallegan. " 'Tis a different tune they'll be givin' whin I marry the girl, eh? Curse the whinin' fools! Look at ould Danny, yander — we'll sind him packin' tomorry, Hanlon!"

" 'Twill be a hard job, thin," flung back the other, "But has the gir-rl agreed to ye, Tom?"

"She will, soon enough. Ye see, I've a sneakin' notion as she's took a likin' to young Sthrang, here. She has but to say yes to me, an' the divil can be takin' him, for all I care. If she says no, into the lake he goes. Then they's the priest; if she says yes, he can stay an' the mission wid him; if not, back home he goes. If she still says no — well, they's other ways yet, Hanlon."

"Plinty, plinty," agreed the old man, with another chuckle. "So it'll be King Gallegan now, eh? But mind this, Tom — go aisy wid ould Danny, Talk wid him, and ye can win him over. He's sthrong wid the oulder men, is Danny, an' 'twould be a bad move just now to be makin' foes whin ye could make fri'nds. Talk wid him, Tom."

"I'll do that," grunted Gallegan, after a brief silence. "I'll do it tonight, Hanlon. Take a deal o' whisky to the lighthouse, mind! If the man can't be made to dhrink, let me know an' we'll fix him —"

"Don't be worryin, Tom. He'll be blind by dark, thrust me for it!"

Clarity was sweeping back into Jim's mind now, and he felt almost a physical sickness at thought of the evil these men were planning. What was more, he knew that he himself was as good as dead, or worse.

Gallegan's grip on the island was tightening with every hour, so much was clear. His purpose in trying to wreck some hapless ship that night grew plainer to Jim; it was not so much in the hope of loot for himself, as in the hope of loot for the islanders. He intended to buy his kingdom with it. If the devilish thing were accomplished successfully, as had been done long ere this, it would be a plain indication to his lawless people that they had one of their own stamp to rule over them, a. man careless of the law and willing to give them rich reward for their support of him.

"They won't see that he's *too* careless of the law," thought Jim to himself. It was easy to imagine what a crowd of whisky-filled men would do that night should a craft be cast ashore. Perhaps Gallegan intended to incriminate them and rule them by fear as well as by favor. He was not lacking in. cunning, certainly!

His intent regarding Jim and Mary McCurdy was practically bound to take successful issue. Gallegan wanted the girl, but he wanted more the dead king's farms and timber. He would have to have this wealth in order to maintain himself in power, and would stop at nothing to obtain it. The schooner was, of course, his for the taking, as was a certain proportion of the rest; but he dared not go too far in open seizure, even as he dared not go too far in banishing Danny Basset abruptly. Jim never believed for a moment that he himself would be set free did Mary consent to become Gallegan's wife. He knew too much. Also, Gallegan would take bitter vengeance for the thrashing

Jim had given him on the highway three days previously.

Taken all in all, Gallegan had everything in his hands. The thought came less bitterly to Jim than he had imagined possible, as he lay helpless to the jolting of the wagon. He began to think that swift punishment had come to him for the wild flame of rage which had sent him into Gallegan with his fists. Yet, except for the sake of Mary McCurdy, Jim cared little who ruled Beaver Island. Had it been possible for him to have swept out Gallegan and his horde and to have replaced them with the Camp Kegomic men, things might have turned out very differently. As it now was, the island mattered nothing to him. , He was alone and unsupported, and had long since given up his wild dream of taking over his father's kingdom. Père Valerius had smashed that into atoms, and rightfully.

Nonetheless, Jim found a remnant of the dream still lingering regretfully in his mind. The tiling would have been rankly impossible while McCurdy lived — he recognized this clearly. With Gallegan reaching for the idle scepter, with the islanders split into factions, and wild misrule bringing havoc in its train, there might have been a possibility of success; but the vision was gone, and Jim's ambition with it. He hated Beaver Island fiercely, and every one upon it, except three people; for Père Valerius he felt sorrow, as the priest seemed doomed to failure; for Danny Basset gratitude, and for Mary McCurdy love. Those three distinctions leaped out vividly in his mind to the jolting of the wagon.

The death of King McCurdy appeared to have unleashed a terrific storm upon the land — an outward sign of the inner turmoil which was following hard upon his passing. The wind howled down upon the long line of wagons, for all the chief families of the island were represented there, and when at length a fine, lashing rain drove upon them the misery of the funeral was complete. Jim's heart ached for the lonely girl somewhere ahead.

Just before reaching town, Hanlon and Gallegan broke into a storm of exultant curses, and as their voices rose slightly Jim found that they had completed an ingenious enough plot for the overthrow of Père Valerius. Immediately the storm was over, Gallegan would take the schooner south and would return with a few families of Holland Dutch from southern Michigan, granting them farms outright. They would have no respect for the priest and would form a solid nucleus for Gallegan's party; the one lacking; element of religious discord would be introduced into the island, and Père Valerius would go the way of all Gallegan's enemies.

"It's clever," reflected Jim angrily, "He must have been doing a lot of thinking in the last day or so! But what's he going to do with me?"

This question soon received a temporary answer. The procession wound around Mount Pisgah amid a driving rainstorm which stilled even the wailing cries of the mourners, and came at last into Saint James. The town had been given over absolutely to the occasion, and the king's body was carried in state to the cleared ground floor of the log-and-frame building which had been King Strang's castle and which McCurdy had converted into a store. The other frame structures of the town were made public property to accommodate the gathered folk.

While those who wished came crowding through the store for a last sight of McCurdy's face, all through the town were proceeding preparations for the great "wake" to be held after the funeral. Canada West and other smuggled liquors were made ready in lavish profusion, for whisky was cheap in Saint James and the occasion was a momentous one, worthy of celebration in such fashion as would be remembered for years to come. On every hand Tom Gallegan was hailed as "king," and no voice was raised against him.

Drenched to the skin and still wrapped in the dirty sacking, Jim was carried from the wagon, up the outside flight of steps behind the store, and to the loft above. This was now crowded with goods removed from the store underneath, and Gallegan ordered him flung on a pile of boxes. The sacking fell away, and Jim obtained one glimpse of the iron mate's exultant face before they left him alone.

The sounds from below rose plainly through the rough boarding, and he was presently aware that McCurdy's body was being carried out to the mission church. Once or twice he heard the rich voice of Père Valerius, then all was lost in a shuffle of feet and the loud cries of the women acting as mourners. Gradually everything died away into silence, and Jim knew that the funeral was taking place.

Vainly he tried to get free of his bonds, but his efforts effected nothing, except that he managed to roll over and so found himself near the tiny paneless opening that served for window to the loft. From this he had a sparse view of the square with its whipping post and the wharf beyond. The *Mary* lay warped in close to the shore, her flag at half-mast. No one was in sight.

The time dragged interminably. The afternoon darkened, and the blast of the storm rose to a shriller and more ominous note. Suddenly there was a scrape of feet, and Jim listened as two men entered the store beneath.

"It was a grand buryin'," one was saying, his tongue thick with liquor. "Did ye see that ould fool Danny Basset cryin' into his oilskins?"

"Aye," growled another. "An' did ye see the gir-rl, eh? They's many a man would be likin' to marry her the day, but Tom's the one, I'm thinkin'. Where's that whisky?"

"Here under the trapdoor. We'll be eatin' at Mither Callyhan's? Glory be, but what a grand eatin' an' dhrinkin' 'twill be tonight!"

"Get that whisky, an' we'll be goin', ye fool. Don't ye know that Tom ordhered ivery one out o' here? He wants to be usin' the place himself the night. Ah, 'tis a grand man, is Tom Gallegan! I hear young Sthrang did be lickin' him the —"

The voices died out with a slam of the door beneath. A man clad in oilskins came into Jim's range of vision, striding down toward the wharf of the schooner. It was almost evening now, and when a storm lantern had been hoisted to the foreyard of the craft to serve as riding light, the man came tramping back and vanished. The noise of feasting echoed dimly through the storm.

Saint James was holding high carnival that night. The loft darkened, and all outside fell into blackness gradually; but Jim could hear the sound of wild voices rising in shouts and snatches of song, and while the storm grew wilder the whisky passed around faster, until the wonder was that there was a sober man left in town. Jim prayed that Mary McCurdy was safe from harm — and prayed again that no ship would come toward the Beavers that night.

More men entered the store space beneath, but Jim could hear nothing of their conversation for the riot of storm and song around. Through the blast pierced the keen scrape of fiddles and the whine of accordions, and he knew that dancing and merriment was in progress, then of a sudden came a new stamp of feet below and a burst of welcome.

"Here he is! Hello, Tom!"

"Have a dhrink, King Gallegan! Whoosh! Here's to yer health —"

"Get to hell out o' here!" snapped Gallegan's hard tones. "I want to use this place, boys. G'wan over to Mother Callahan's and join the dancin', will ye?"

The men stamped out, singing and yelling drunkenly. Jim noted, however, that Gallegan seemed quite sober. The door slammed.

"Did ye 'tend to him, Hanlon? I see they's no light goin'."

"I did that," came Hanlon's evil chuckle. "He's dead dhrunk, Tom — an' I'm not so far from it me own silf! Losh, losh — what a blissid night it is! But, Tom! I'll tell ye something'."

"What is it?"

"Git ould Danny over here quick. One o' the b'ys was dhrunk an' did be tellin' him ye had took young Sthrang an' hild him up beyand."

A savage curse broke from Gallegan.

"Where's the old fool?"

"Over at McGuire's. He'll be makin' throuble, Tom, unless ye sittle him the night. He's talkin' free about how the gir-rl shud have McCurdy's place and —"

"I'll settle him!" snapped Gallegan. "You're right, Hanlon, I'll have to be shuttin' his mouth one way or another, an' quick about it. I —"

Even where he lay above, Jim could hear the wild blast of. wind and rain enter as the door was opened suddenly and a new voice broke in:

"Tom! For the love o' God come along wid us!"

"Eh ? What the divil's happened?"

"They's a three-master dhrivin' in at the south cliff, undher the false light, Tom! Sind the b'ys wid some whisky or —"

"Hanlon!" leaped out Gallegan's roar. "Spread the word an' get down there wid every one ye can raise. Yell know what to do. I'll have to get hold o' Danny first, an' shut his damned mouth, so you go ahead. I'll be right down after ye."

All three went rushing forth into the night, and Jim could hear a confused noise of shouts and stamping feet as the news of the wreck spread abroad and the half-maudlin crew went off for the cliffs. Tight-lipped and despairing, Jim stared into the darkness and hoped against hope that the "three-master" might perceive the lure and yet draw into the harbor shelter.

Gallegan had risen to the occasion better than Jim had looked for, from his knowledge of the mate. He had kept sober evidently, and fully realized the importance of securing Danny Basset's silence. Danny knew too much, and to have an open enemy about when such devil's work was forward would be rank suicide, as the mate had seen.

Now Jim heard a stamp of hoofs and a creaking of wagons, while through his narrow range of vision flitted lanterns and oilskin-clad figures. How many hours had passed he did not know, but the night could not be very far onward since the storm had brought down premature darkness in its train. A single wild whisky-laden yell smote in from outside:

"On the rocks, b'ys! Down wid ye!"

The door below opened again, and feet stamped in. There came a loud voice, as though a man passing by had seen the figures inside and paused to shout at them.

"Hey, Tom! Ain't ye comin' down? Iverybody's pilin' out — come along! Where's the praste?"

"Locked up with McCurdy's girl!" roared Gallegan's voice. "G'wan — I'll be down soon enough — I got to talk to Danny, here."

The door slammed noisily, shaking the whole rude building. Then rose a familiar wheeze that sent a thrill through the helpless Jim: "Well, Tom? Did ye be wantin' to talk wid ould Danny?"

CHAPTER XV
AND WAS DELIVERED OUT OF BONDAGE

Jim strained himself to listen. He tried to thump his bound hands and feet on the boxes, but vainly. Danny knew that he lay up here helpless, for Hanlon had said as much.

He groaned inwardly and lay quiet, knowing Danny could do nothing. Picturing to himself the scene below — the red-shocked, watery-eyed old man facing the cold, hard Gallegan, he knew only too well that he could look for no aid. What he forgot was that every man has his great moment, whether he be cook or woodsman, or of even lesser estate.

"Yes," responded Gallegan, "an' I've got little enough time to be wastin' on the likes o' you, Danny Basset. I want to know where ye stand, an' quick about it."

"I'm standin' here right now," returned Danny, with a wheezy chuckle. "What do ye mane, Tom?"

"I mean this. Are you for or against me? Ye know too much, Danny, an' I'm not trustin' ye, that's flat. I've got young Strang where I want him; I've got the kingship here, and I'll be keepin' it. And —"

"And ye've got a ship on the cliffs beyand," broke in Danny, his voice suddenly firmer than Jim had ever heard it before. "They's poor, hilpless men beatin' on thim rocks, Tom Gallegan, goin' to their death be your work. That's what ye mane, ain't it? Yell be wantin' to know if ould Danny's goin' to kape his mouth shut or not, eh?"

"That's about it," and Gallegan laughed harshly. "Ye're no fool, Danny, in spite of your looks! They's none here to be interferin' with me now; Jim Strang's safe, the tax man's been shipped back — God bring him safe to Petoskey! — an' Beaver Island's mine."

"Thrue for ye, Tom Gallegan," and at the hesitation evident in Danny's voice Jim felt a cold finger of fear touch upon him. Was it possible, after all, that Danny would be frightened into giving his allegiance? "Thin what do ye want o' me?"

"No more o' your blarney," answered Gallegan roughly, as a faint chorus of drunken yells came down the rushing blast. "Yes or no, an' quick! Are ye for me or agin' me, Danny Basset?"

Jim listened, every nerve tensed, for the answer. For a moment none came. He heard an almost inaudible tinkling thud, as though a glass had fallen on the earthen floor below and broken. Then in startling sequence rose a low, muffled groan, and silence.

"God forgive me! I'm agin' ye, Tom Gallegan!" came Danny's wheeze.

What had happened down below? Jim writhed in his bonds at the thought. The next instant he heard the door slam shut, and feet stumbled on the outer stairs leading to the loft from behind. A dim lantern light diffused itself through the loft as a figure entered and held the light overhead.

"Jim! Where are ye, me lad?"

Danny caught sight of the motionless form on the boxes, and ran forward with his knife open. Setting down the lantern, he cut carefully at Jim's bonds, his fingers trembling and his face ghastly to look upon.

"God forgive me!" he muttered fearfully, "I hit him wid an impty bottle!"

Half strangled by his gag, Jim sat up. He tried to clasp the old man's hand, but hands and feet were useless temporarily from the tight ropes, while his wounded leg throbbed with blood pressed back.

"They's no time to be wastin'!" cried Danny hastily, starting up and going to the tiny square of the window. "Look, me lad!"

Jim stooped. Following the shaking finger, he saw a twinkling light out beyond the harbor entrance — another ship was driving in to disaster! He tried to stand, but fell forward, clutching at the boxes.

"I — I can't walk, Danny!" he panted hoarsely. "Get out to the lighthouse quick —"

Danny whirled with a rustle of dripping oilskins, and clumped away hurriedly. In a frenzy of impatience, Jim rubbed ankles and wrists. The moments seemed like hours. Again he tried to walk, as new life flooded into his ankles, only to go pitching forward into the boxes once more with a despairing cry.

Would the old man reach the lighthouse in time to save this second vessel? Jim groaned. He knew now what had happened below, and his own helplessness appalled him. In desperation he rubbed at his ankles, and at length pulled himself up. He staggered, but held firm.

Catching up the lantern Danny had left, he got to the door. Every step was torture, but when he stood on the outside stairs his numbed feet were stronger beneath him; and at length he reached the corner of the building. He stood irresolute for a moment, while the wild fury of wind swept on him with a driving rain. What was to be done?

Danny was gone to the lighthouse, which stood out on the sandy spit to the north of the harbor, and he would be able to attend to the light without help. Jim strained his eyes through the murk for some sight of the vessel, and uttered a cry of joy as he saw the tossing light again. She seemed to be some ship beating in against the storm from the south — perhaps a lumber schooner from Harbor Springs, running for shelter.

With this, he remembered Gallegan, and turned. If Danny had knocked the man out, he must be secured at once. Then there was Père Valerius, whom Gallegan had seemingly locked in one of the houses to provide against interference, and Mary. They would have to get somewhere away from the drink-maddened crowd of islanders, perhaps back to the McCurdy farm, until they could get away from the island together.

Leaning against the wind, he stumbled forward to the front corner of the building and edged around to the door. He drew it open and plunged inside, the wind slamming it behind him with furious force. Jim held up the lantern.

There was a large draped platform of barrels and boards in the center of the room, doubtless where the body of McCurdy had lain that afternoon. Stretched on the floor beside one corner of it lay Gallegan, Blood was flowing from a jagged cut in his head, and beside him were the shattered fragments of an empty whisky bottle. Danny must have struck like a flash, and with terrific force.

For an instant Jim fancied that the iron mate was dead. Kneeling, he pulled up the man's head and felt for his heart. Relief surged over him as he felt a faint beat, and with that he dropped Gallegan and rose to his feet. His enemy was safe for the present, and there were other things to attend to.

Catching up one of the bottles from the platform, he swallowed a little of the fiery liquor, and it gave him new strength. If he could find the priest and Mary, they could go aboard the vessel which was now beating in, and could hold off the islanders until morning, or until the storm was blown out. With this thought, he stripped away Gallegan's oilskins and donned them over his wet clothes, more for warmth than protection, left the lantern where it was, and stumbled out into the storm again.

He had no idea where Père Valerius was locked, and stepped out to look around. A cry of joy broke from him as a sudden clear beam of light shot athwart the storm from the northern spit; Danny had started the light! Jim turned, only to bump abruptly into a heavy figure; before he could cry out, two terrible hands went to his throat and he was lifted from his feet and shaken.

Frantic, desperate, Jim broke the hold. He saw a vague figure to one side, and gripped it in a clinch to gain time.

"Help — father —"

"Mary!"

Jim released her, incredulous. At the same instant a hand fell on his shoulder, and in the blackness he caught answering words of amazement from his assailant:

"You, Jim? Ah, I took you for one of —"

"Here, get back inside the building!" cried Jim hastily. He realized that he had met those whom he sought, and wasted no time talking. "We'll have to move lively. Gallegan's in there — Danny smashed him."

Drawing them back with him, he flung open the door of the store and hurriedly pushed them inside. Catching up the shrinking girl, he placed her on the platform where she could not see the smitten mate. Père Valerius knelt over Gallegan, then rose.

"He is but stunned. And you, my son? Where have you been?"

Jim stared in blank amazement. Mary was wrapped in an oilskin coat, but the other figure was drenched, the brown robe tattered and muddy, the face bruised and cut. His eyes went back to the girl, and at sight of her wan face and cold gaze he repressed with savage restraint the eagerness which leaped up in him.

"Danny was here —" and he briefly related what had chanced since his capture, telling of his own release. "Danny should be back soon. We can get aboard that boat coming in, and we might take Gallegan along. He'll have much to answer for —"

"These poor, deluded people will have much to answer for also," and a sad smile lighted the bruised face of the priest. "Danny set me free also, my son, and I hastened down the cliffs to try and stop what was forward. Ah — it was terrible — terrible!"

The man's face reflected the horror of his thought, and he twisted his strong white hands in impotent agony.

"Pray God you may never see such a sight as I saw this night, James Strang! Men and women were there, clustered about the fires, reeling and shouting in drunken frenzy; out in the darkness a schooner was breaking up and her cargo drifting in on the rocks. I twice saw the forms of men borne to safety, only to be dashed back by the hands of other men who had no mercy. They are down there this instant, loading their spoil into wagons, dancing around the fires, exulting over the poor wretches whose goods they have thieved — ah, God forgive them, God forgive them!"

"But you?" cried Jim, wondering. "What happened —"

"They turned upon me. I tried to stop them, tried to save some of those poor castaways — they stoned me and drove me away with curses and blasphemies. God forgive them as I do; they were drunk, men and women alike. So I came back, hoping to get away with you and Mary, if at all possible or —"

The priest sank down, his face in his hands, completely overborne by the horror of that night. Jim turned to the girl. He was calm now, well poised and vibrant with power, as he realized that the situation lay in his own hands. The merry, gay-hearted boy had been crushed away, and he was left a man — pale, stern, conscious of the mastery which lay within him and the miracle of change which had been wrought in his spirit through many sorrows.

"Mary," he said simply, "won't you forget what's between us, and just trust me until we —"

"My trust in you is shattered!" she broke in coldly.

"But — Mary!" and all his desperate longing leaped out in eye and voice. "Can't you understand that I was only trying to help that poor girl —"

"Don't lie to me!" she said wearily, disdain in her eyes. "I saw her in your arms. That was enough, Jim. I can't believe the story you tell, after what I saw and heard; it's too far-fetched, too improbable — oh, leave me alone, leave me alone!"

Jim found the priest's hand on his arm, and turned to catch a look of warning.

"Come, my son — we have other things to attend to now. Your idea of going aboard this ship was good. Mary, will you not let Jim take you to Little Traverse? Will you not trust him so far at my bidding? You and he and Danny can go together —"

"Eh?" exclaimed Jim. "And you, then — surely you'll not remain here after what those devils have done to you this night?"

"They have but the more need of me, and the mission here is in my charge." The priest's face was calm, and its sadness only intensified the stern will which underlay all. "When these people have recovered from the frenzied madness of drink, then will be the time for my work to bear fruit among them. The shipwrecked men yonder will not have died in vain; if I know the hearts of men, these islanders will have sore need of all the spiritual comfort I can give them, my son. There will never be another ship wrecked upon these shores — remember, my errand is to bear light into the dark places!"

Jim was silent, for he understood — though a month previously he would have been far from understanding. Turning, he took up some of the food which had been left on the table for

Gallegan's use; he had not eaten since morn, and felt the need of sustenance.

"Eat something," and Père Valerius addressed Mary with quiet authority. "You have tasted nothing today, my child, and you must not let grief weaken you."

She obeyed, obviously forcing herself to the task. It was a bitter meal for Jim also, and a strange one — standing there in the house his father had built, with the storm shrieking down outside and Gallegan lying under his feet, still unconscious. In the midst there came a step at the door, and Danny Basset entered, shivering with cold.

"Glory be!" panted the old man, on seeing them. He swung off his oilskin hat with a slosh of water and sank breathlessly against the side of the platform. His eyes fell on Gallegan, and he started suddenly. "He's not dead, your riverince?"

"Not a bit of it," smiled the priest, "though you struck hard enough."

"Faith," and Danny uttered a wheezy sigh of relief, "I was so scart I wouldn't be knockin' him out wid one blow — well, let be. So all's well an' sound?"

"So far," grunted Jim. "Is that ship coming in? What is she?"

"Divil a bit do I know, me lad. She looks like a bit of a schooner, an' she's beatin' up the harbor this minute toward the wharf. 'Tis a glad man I am they's no murder on me sowl this night!" And he glanced down at Gallegan, his watery-blue eyes blinking.

Jim related what had taken place, and set forth his plan as regarded going aboard the incoming vessel, Danny looked from face to face, hesitant.

"So ye'll not go, your riverince? Well, mebbe I could da worse than be stoppin' wid ye. I've me own bit of farm to be lookin' to —"

"Why, Danny!" The girl suddenly lost her apathy. Slipping to the floor, she seized the old man's arm, "You'll go along to take care of me, won't you?"

"Sure, darlin', if ye're wantin' me," and Danny gunned widely at the success of his little stratagem. "What's to be done, father?"

"You and Jim had better go aboard the ship with Mary," replied the priest slowly. "Take her to Little Traverse or Mackinac, wherever the ship goes, and put her in charge of the priest until I send for her again —"

"I don't want to come back here!" broke out the girl bitterly. "I never want to see the place again! I tried to stand it while father was alive, but now —"

"Well, we'd better be moving down to the wharf," said Jim quietly. "When the islanders see the light is going again, they'll be flocking back here in short order. You two bring Mary, and I'll go on ahead to help line in the boat."

Catching up the lantern, he left them to follow and started for the wharf. The rain had ceased, but the wind was howling down wildly; fighting his way against it, Jim hastened out to receive the schooner, now edging up to the end of the long wharf. A moment later he was between the huge stacked piles of firewood which lined the wharf and shut off the sight of what lay beyond.

He caught a shrill yell from ahead, and broke into a run; as he cleared the last pile of firewood, he came upon a wild scene which halted him abruptly. The end of the wharf was black with men; more were piling out of the schooner with lanterns, whose yellow light shone on rifle barrels, axes, and cant hooks. Even as his figure came into the light, a mad burst of voices took up a song and sent it lurching down the blast:

> "— he's put de calks to de Irishman!
> He's bus' de jail at Pierre le Gran',
> He's lose one eye an' bees ear's been tore,
> But hees fits' she's split dat — big — jail — door!
> An' de Irish run when he's look for more,
> For he's take hees w'isky clear.
> By gar!" He's take hees w'isky clear!"

And the crowd surged about Jim with a long howl of triumph. The raiders had come.

CHAPTER XVI
HOW A MAN WAS TEMPTED

For a space Jim was absolutely beyond speech. The fact that his friends were here was overwhelming; the surprise of it was paralyzing.

The singing, cheering, cursing men surged out on the wharf and surrounded him; until some fifty-odd were gathered in a solid mass. There was huge-bearded Antoine Macfarlan, double splay-bladed ax in hand; rat-faced George St. Peter, bearing a rifle; Jean Tache's red shock of hair gleamed out, Henri Gilbault, gaunt and fierce-eyed, shoved men aside with his peavey — all the woods leaders save one, for whom Jim looked in vain.

"But — but — what's it all mean?" gasped Jim, weary with hand-shaking and deafened by the mad yellin".

De Irish — dey go like dat!" and Gilbault snapped his fingers excitedly.

"Where's McCurdy?" demanded Antoine suddenly. The crowd took up the words in a fierce yell of utter savagery. "Where's dat dam McCurdy?"

"Dead," returned Jim, his eyes hard. "Keep your tongues off him."

The words passed around, and a staring silence ensued. In a few words Jim told them how the king had died, and was even then under the ground.

"What's happened?" he asked, when the tale was done. "What got you over here?"

"What?" exploded big Antoine, bringing down his ax with a resounding thump on the wharf. "You know 'bout Marc, mebbe? He's been beat up — mos' dead, Jim! He's in de hospital now — Little Traverse. Dat girl Leny, she's bring him back, tell us 'bout you an' dat dam Gallegan. We hear 'bout you an' Marc, dis mornin' we come to Little Traverse, we take de schooner an' come to kill dat dam Gallegan an' make de raid sure."

A low, savage mutter, infinitely more menacing than the shouts which had preceded it, swept through the mass of men. Jim understood now, and exulted. The story of Marc's maltreatment had spread through the woods like wildfire, and the woodsmen had poured down to Little Traverse in an avenging torrent. Jim compressed his lips; history had indeed repeated itself!

"We don' care what de bon père say!" shouted Jean Tache suddenly. "We come for raid dem dam Irish! You all right, Jim?"

"Yes," nodded Jim shortly. "I'm all right."

So Leny had raised the woodsmen, then! He made swift inquiry for her, and Antoine shook his head, passing over a folded paper.

"She's not come, Jim. She's send you dis paper."

Jim nodded and thrust it into his pocket. Somewhere behind in the darkness, shut off by the mob, were the priest, Danny, and Mary. But he realized something more important still. Upon that moment hung the issue. These men were swaying in the leash, and were out of his control for the time being; he must either reassert the authority he had dropped that night in Camp Kegomic, or else they would brush him aside and sweep out across the island in a savage horde.

He knew these men, and read murder in their faces. They were not to be checked or restrained by Père Valerius this time. If they found Gallegan, the iron mate would get short shrift; and for all his hatred, Jim knew he must save Gallegan, if possible. The woodsmen had taken the law into their own hands — but the issue lay with him. His was the vision, his the dream, his the voice which had awakened them in the first place. Unless he could hold in check the storm he had raised, there would be bitter responsibility upon his shoulders. Yet — why should he check it, after all? Whose was the kingdom now?

"Père Valerius! Danny! Let 'em through, you men."

In wondering silence, the men shoved aside to let Père Valerius stride through with Danny after him. Mary clung to the old man in affright, but Jim paid them no heed. He turned to St. Peter and Jean Tache, the bitterest of the woods leaders.

"Take the men around to the south cliffs, George and Jean. Danny Basset, here, will guide you — don't fear to trust him. Gallegan has wrecked a schooner down there. Try and save what lives you can, and round up all Gallegan's crowd. No fighting, remember — round them up and bring 'em back to town, prisoners."

He motioned the two leaders to be off, and the men streamed away after them with one terribly savage yell. Jim whirled on the others, who would have followed.

"Wait! Come down to the cabin with me, boys. Henri, is there a spare cabin aboard here for Miss McCurdy?"

"Yes," returned Gilbault "Plenty, Jim. I'm take her safe."

The girl shrank back from Jim's extended hand, but with a look into the gaunt face of Gilbault, she obeyed the priest's nod and stepped aboard the schooner.

As the leaders tramped aft, Jim drew a long sigh of relief. So far, then, he was firmly in the saddle, Père Valerius, seeming perfectly cognizant of what was forward, took his arm and they walked aft together in silence. Descending to the large mess cabin, they found the leaders grouped about the table beneath the swinging lights.

The arrival had been opportune, as Jim could not but admit. At the same time, he had seen too much of the excesses of maddened men that night; he felt he could not loose this storm of savage hatred upon the island. The very fact that these men had crossed from Little Traverse in the teeth of a raging gale showed they were beyond all reasoning.

Henri Gilbault came in, and took his seat with a nod of reassurance to Jim. Antoine, who was evidently the head of the party, plucked at his great beard and spoke.

"Is de king dead, Père Valerius? If it's true, we make Jim de king."

The priest glanced about, then told quietly of McCurdy's death and burial, and of the events immediately fallowing. When he finished, Antoine looked at him sourly.

"Tell me somet'ing," he rumbled, with slow determination. "Back at Camp Kegomic you make de fool of us. Mebbe you were right den. But now — no! Mebbe you find out somet'ing since den,'oui! Mebbe you learn somet'ing 'bout dis Gallegan, eh? Now we come over to kill dis dam Gallegan, père. Dat be sure; we do dat tonight, by gar!"

He paused at a swift, eager murmur from the rest, then continued: "You tell me dis, Père Valerius. When we take de farm, de sawmill, de boat — when we turn out de dam Irish; what den? Mebbe de law give us hell, mebbe not. You tell me dis: shall we make Jim de king?"

Père Valerius gazed steadily at him for a moment.

"You are determined on this raid, Antoine Macfarlan?"

The hoarse mutter which broke from every throat was answer enough.

"Then this is my answer," and the priest spoke with quiet deliberation. "Events have changed greatly, my sons, since I met you at Camp Kegomic. Then I told you your idea was a mad thing, and I was right. Now it is different, Gallegan has outraged himself this night before God and man, as have his followers. If you can make James Strang king of this island, as I believe you can — then do it!"

The woodsmen, who had been eying Jim's strangely altered features with no small interest, broke out into a storm of applause. Père Valerius quieted them with upraised hand. The kindliness of his brown eyes died to a stern scrutiny of each man in turn. "But mind this! If you do to these people as they did to the Mormons who lived here before them, you will rue it bitterly. If you take their farms and wealth, if you turn them out naked into the world, you will rue it!

This is all I have to say. As to Jim Strang, give him the king's title. It would be the salvation of this island."

Before his words, the unveiled hostility of the circle melted away. Jim sat in staring amazement, knowing that Père Valerius was sincere beyond a doubt, yet fully as surprised as the rest. He had expected a hard battle with the priest.

"By gar!" ejaculated Antoine slowly, "By gar!"

"Listen to me, all of you!"

Jim sprang to his feet, his mop of red-gold hair blazing even as his eyes blazed in the lamplight, and his face settling into hard, grim lines. He must show himself master of these men now — or never. Sentiment was swept away. They had come to avenge him and Marc, but the snarl of the beast was creeping through, and either his or another hand would grip them and use the".

Let the kingship wait for a moment, my friends. You have acknowledged that I am your leader — and I mean to be obeyed. Understand that? *Obeyed!* Except by my own orders, not a farm on this island shall be taken, not a person injured, not a bit of loot brought aboard this schooner. What is done shall be done through me alone, not through you. It is your own choice; now dispute it if you dare! Am I your leader or not?"

They stared up at him during a long moment, silent before the fierce tensity of his face, the iron dominance of his will. Antoine cleared his throat.

"What you want to do?"

"What's that to you?" Jim fairly shot the savage words at him. "If you don't intend to obey me, say so and I wash my hands of you. If you do — then you'll obey."

He read their answer in their eyes. He had conquered.

There had been method behind those swift words, for he had remembered Gallegan, and the memory intruded upon his thrilling triumph with a deeper note of fear. He must get the man somewhere to safety.

"I'll be back in a moment — wait here," he snapped, and strode to the companionway.

Reaching the deck, he went to the rigging and ascended a few feet until he could peer above the piled firewood at the town. A few scattered lights were visible, but he could hear nothing; raiders and the raided were swallowed up in the black night. Under the stern of the schooner was a dull, slow thumping, and he saw a fish boat with mounted mast lined to the wharf. The mast was banging against schooner and spiles. On the other side the wharf lay the deserted *Mary*.

Jim dropped to the wharf. As he did so, there drifted down the wind one faint yell, so instinct with wild ferocity that he shivered. Instantly he started up the long wharf on the run, dreading what he might come upon.

At the wharf's head he found it — a little group of figures pushing down, who greeted him with another ringing yell of brutal savagery. The foremost figure was that of Wabanasso, an Indian woodsman who worked at Kegomic, though owning a large tract of timber in his own right.

"Jim! We got him!"

In the darkness he could see the figure they dragged along, and a deep curse told him that Tom Gallegan still lived and fought There was but one course to take; if he ordered the mate released, he would never be obeyed.

"Bring him along to the cabin, boys; but don't hurt him."

Jim turned and strode back. If he was to save his enemy from the rabid hatred of these woodsmen, he must fight with all his weapons. When he came back into the cabin, a swift plan had flashed into his mind, and he broke the news bluntly:

"They've got Gallegan. He'll be here in a minute."

He caught one swift glance from Père Valerius, then came the stamp of feet on the decks, and with a running growl of curses the woods leaders swept to their feet as Gallegan was pushed in and fell sprawling beside the table. Wabanasso jerked him up again.

The iron mate looked around defiantly, blood from his cut head still black on his cheek. When he saw that ring of savage faces, the snarling lips, the maddened eyes, he went livid; in that terrible moment he must have realized exactly what had happened. Antoine heaved up his great ax, murder stark upon his face.

"Wait!" Jim leaped at him, tore away the ax, flung it on the table with a crash. "Sit down, you! All of you!"

They hesitated, growling at him like dogs pushed back from their prey. Then they obeyed slowly.

"Who has the greater right to vengeance on this man — you or me?" demanded Jim fiercely. "He murdered Alec — was Alec more to you or to me?"

"You," grunted Antoine sullenly. The others nodded.

"Then that vengeance is not yours to take, but mine," continued Jim swiftly. "Gallegan has pursued me with his mockery and hate — not you. He and his men beat up Marc, and if Marc isn't here, then I'll take the vengeance for that — not you."

"Dat's right," spoke up Gilbault. "You kill him for Marc, Jim."

"I shall take my own revenge on this man," said Jim sternly, searching their faces. "You agree that it is mine to take?"

Man after man nodded. Gallegan's breast was heaving, and he looked around like a hunted animal, but without cringing. The sight of that agonized face was too much for Père Valerius, who came to his feet with a low cry.

"My son — what would you do?"

"Go into that after cabin and see." Jim pointed to the door behind, then turned to the big Indian. "Wabanasso, take him in there."

One snarling cry broke from Gallegan as the Indian caught his bound arms and shoved him forward; Jim plucked up Antoine's big ax from the table, then followed with Père Valerius. He brought one of the swinging lanterns and hung it to a hook in the cabin.

"Go outside," he directed the Indian. "I'll do the rest"

Wabanasso's white teeth flashed out, he withdrew, and the door slammed. Gallegan lay on the floor where he had been flung in a crumpled heap. Crossing to the prostrate figure, Jim cut his bonds with the ax, then took him by the shoulder and heaved him up before the stern window of the schooner.

"There's a boat down there," he said abruptly, half snarling; this vengeance of his was a harder thing than he had thought, for he hated Gallegan bitterly. "You can't get away by the shore, or they'd hunt you into every corner of the island. Slide down into that boat and you can make the harbor mouth in one tack. Then you'll have to take your chance with the storm — and I don't give a damn whether you swim or sink. Get out!"

Shivering, Gallegan drew himself up. He looked into Jim's white, hard face and then turned away from the open window. The man seemed suddenly bowed together, stricken into a ghastly travesty of his strength — yet he was unbroken.

"To hell wid you an' your mercy!" he growled, facing Jim. "I'll take my chance wid thim divils o' yourn —"

Infuriated, Jim shook him savagely.

"You fool! Do you want to be torn in pieces?"

Lending emphasis to his words, a great stamping of feet resounded along the wharf outside — the raiders were returning. There came a sound of shouts and yells and curses blending into one deep roar of maddened voices. Gallegan lost the final remnant of his defiance, a groan broke from him, and without a word more he went to the window and climbed out into the night. He was gone.

"Ah, my son — —"

"Be quiet!" Jim turned on the priest with eyes which struck the other silent. "Tell me — is it your real wish that I take the kingship? Quick, man!"

The priest nodded. "Yes."

Jim answered nothing, but strode to the door. Stepping into the cabin, he saw St. Peter and Jean Tache returned, talking excitedly. An eager rush of voices leaped at him.

"Where is he? What you do, Jim? You make for —"

"Shut up!" lashed out Jim. "Jean, what did you and George do?"

"We save two men," returned the awed Jean Tache. "We got dem dam Irish, Jim, an' tied 'em up an' lock 'em in de house, men an' women. All drunk," and he spat in disgust.

"Keep 'em safe, then. Now, boys, I took my revenge on Gallegan — a revenge he'll never forget. No, don't ask what it was — I'll not tell you yet. He's gone; let that do you."

At these ambiguous words, a yell of applause shrilled up. Antoine leaped to his feet with a roar:

"Who's be de king now? King Jim!"

"King Jim! King Jim!"

A great shout rocked the schooner, spread to the men on deck and wharf, thrilled up to the town, and was answered by the men on guard over their captives. Jim looked around, flushed with triumph, so wild an exultation surging over him that he could not speak.

In that instant he saw how all things lay in his hand. Gallegan's chief men were prisoners, to be dealt with by law. He himself was master. The influence of the Beaver Island vote meant practical independence — and he could wield it by the help of these men! All misrule and violence could be banished, French and Irish and Indian could be banded together in harmony, Beaver Island could be made a real kingdom — and he could do it!

Suddenly, as his hands clenched in his pockets, his lingers touched a folded paper. He remembered the note Antoine had brought him from Leny. Striving for a calm mastery of himself under those watching eyes, he brought it forth and opened it. It was written in pencil, and he held it to the light, trying to read the ugly scrawl.

Deer Jim:

Im at Littel Traverse and Iv rased hell over heer. I hope Antone does what he says hell do. Jim. I no I aint a good girl and Im dam sorry about what took plase in the cav. I gess Mary thot you was lovin me and I wisht you had bin Jim. I love you but I no I aint your kind. I no you love Mary and I hope she aint mad no more. Im goin to find that feler you told me about. Jim I gess hes my pa all rite. If I find him Im goin to be a good girl and you wont see me no more. Goodby Jim. You bin dam good to me and Im goin to think of you and be a good girl now. I hope Mary ain't mad no more. Goodby Jim.

Leny.

The pitiful words ran into a blur before Jim's eyes. He gazed long at the paper, then shoved it quickly into the hand of Antoine. "Give it to Mary McCurdy — wake her up — tell her where it came from," he said huskily, all his vision forgotten. Antoine stared at him.

"But Jim — you'll be de king?"

The words met with an echoing murmur, from the rest. Jim looked at the perplexed woodsmen, then turned hastily toward the after cabin, shoving Père Valerius aside.

"Wait!" he commanded, keeping down a quiver in his voice. "Wait, boys — leave me alone for a while. I've got to think about something — I'll be back —"

And, entering, the cabin, he shut the door.

CHAPTER XVII
AND THE DAWN MADE ANSWER

How long Jim remained alone in the after cabin he never knew, but it must have been hours, for the oil in his lamp began to flicker ere he had left. Jim was thinking as he had never thought in all his life; he scanned everything point by point, desperately wrestling with his temptation until he found the answer. Just as the first vague gray of dawn stole through the window, he found it; and with swift pencil and paper he put his answer into words.

Barely had he finished when he was aware of a timid knock on the cabin door. There had been others, but he had let them pass unheeded. Now he rose quickly, unbarred the door, and flung it open to admit — Mary McCurdy.

For a moment their eyes met in silence. Then, while he closed the door, she passed him and turned. He saw a folded paper in her hand, and knew it for Leny's letter.

"Jim!" she spoke softly, and her hands went out to his. "I — I know now. I talked to the men — I found out how wrong I had been. This letter was —"

But that pitiful little letter was suddenly crushed. The girl would have shrunk away, but Jim laughed once and caught her, a great glory in his face as he drank of her eyes.

"I knew — I knew!" he cried swiftly. "I knew when I read that note that you could not doubt it! And now — you've come back to me — we will go away together and you will marry me some day?"

"If you still want me —"

Her words were lost in Jim's folding arms.

"Come!" he said, after a moment, and lifted his head.

Opening the door, he led her out. In the mess cabin he found some of the men asleep over the long table. Waking them, he ordered them to gather the others on the wharf; then, looking down at the paper on which he had written, he went over his answer word by word and found it good. With a smile into the girl's wondering eyes, he led her to the companionway and so out on deck amid the gathering woodsmen.

Still holding his hand, she mounted the rail beside him and dropped to the wharf. The men were assembling by lantern light; one after another Jim greeted the leaders, passed a "b'jou" with them all, smiled silently into the questioning eyes of Père Valerius, and when quiet had fallen upon the men, addressed them abruptly.

"Boys, Mary McCurdy's going to many me."

An instant of amazed muteness, then the astounded woodsmen began to roar out wild applause. Jim checked them

"Wait! Now, Mary, you know who these friends of ours are, and how they've come to make me king in your father's place. After we're married, shall we live here —"

"No — not that!" she broke in quickly, imploringly, forgetting the men around.

"I want to go away from here and never see Beaver Island again —"

"But your wealth is all here, your father's farms and timber!"

She drew away from him, her sea-blue eyes flashing up.

"What! Do you think I would touch that wealth, Jim? You should know me better than that! I've heard too much about it since I came home — how it was taken from those poor Mormons, of the pain and suffering and ruin it cost! I would sooner starve than eat another piece of bread earned by the tears of so many people. Take it if you want it — whoever wants that stolen wealth can have it, for I'll never set foot on that land again as long as I live!"

The wan tragedy in her face struck them all silent, even Jim. He had not quite guessed how deeply she felt the bitterness of her father's possessions, but he was not sorry that he had drawn the swift outburst from her. Quietly taking her hand once more, he turned to the men.

"Well, boys, you've heard how she feels about it. Wabanasso — are you there?"

"I'm here, Jim." The big Indian stepped out in no little wonder. The dawn was slowly lightening over the harbor

"Wabanasso, last year you wanted to swap your timber near Camp Kegomic for that forty acres of cleared land belonging to Alec. Does the offer still hold good?"

The brown face wrinkled up in perplexity.

"Huh? What you want, Jim?"

"Straight business I'm offering to swap with you. Yes or no?"

"Huh! I want good farm — yes."

"Fine!" Jim's voice rang out in a great laugh, and his eyes went to the mass of puzzled, bewildered faces which hemmed him in. "Antoine, that land of Wabanasso's joins on your cedar up beyond the camp. Want to take me in as partner?"

"Look here, Jim, what you mean?" The giant frowned in anxious wonder as he stared at Jim. "We ain't talkin' about dis timber. We want for make you king here. You say yes, den we go t'rough dis Island —"

"You answer my question," smiled Jim. "Want me for partner? Yes or no?"

"Yes," growled Antoine helplessly.

"All right. Danny Basset — where are you?"

Old Danny stood forth with a wide grin. Surveying him, Jim read cunning understanding in the watery-blue eyes, and knew Danny had guessed his inten".

Danny, do you want to cross to the mainland? Mary and I will be married some day, and there's a place for you in our timber camp if you want it."

"Ah, me lad, none o' your jokin' now!" wheezed Danny reproachfully. "Sure, wasn't that all settled an' done wid last night, now?"

Jim smiled again as he met the gaze of Père Valerius. He was very sure of himself now. That very fact perplexed the crowd all the more. The woodsmen could not understand what he was driving at, and said so openly; the voice of Antoine lifted across the uneasy mutter, and the big camp boss stepped forward angrily.

"Jim! What you tryin' to do? We come here to make you de king. Why you talk 'bout dis timber business? We got no time to waste, Jim. We mus' go down de island quick, catch dem dam Irish —"

Then Jim told them of how he had avenged himself on Tom Gallegan. His words met with stark incredulity. They would not, could not believe him until Père Valerius confirmed his statement, and at this Jim thought he would be struck down and mobbed. Storming out curses and reproaches, utterly infuriated, the men surged around in a wild mass, brandishing their motley weapons and filling the morning with bitter imprecation, while the girl shrank closer to him in trembling fear.

Gradually their rage burned itself out into a sullen discontent. Jim, who had faced them with steady, unwavering eyes, stepped to the rail of the schooner and looked them over with a faint smile. Once more he mastered them by sheer force of his will and personality.

"Boys," and his voice rang clear and firm, "I freed Gallegan for the same reason that there'll be no raid today. You forget what Père Valerius said to us that night at Camp Kegomic; I had almost forgotten it myself, but it's true. Wrong does not right wrong, boys. If we were to carry out this raid, we wouldn't gain by it. First, those of you who have come to get farms and loot, go help yourselves to King McCurdy's, for his daughter holds the only title and she will have none of it. Hurry up, now — go and help yourselves, those of you who wish. It's not with you I want to speak, but with the others. Get along with you — hurry! Now's your chance, so don't miss it."

The men read earnestness in his face and words. Half a dozen of them edged through the crowd and vanished up the wharf. The others waited, immobile, fascinated by wonder and curiosity, a mingling of bewilderment and menace in their faces. "We've got a gang of wreckers in the town, there," went on Jim quietly, "and they'll have to be taken over to Charlevoix and held for trial. That brings up one reason why we couldn't turn out the Irish — because of the law. Sooner or later the sheriff would jump you, and even if you settled half the island there would be a continual feud between us and the Irish settlers."

"But if you're de king," broke in Antoine, plucking at his beard, "den you be —"

"No, I couldn't keep peace. Neither my father nor King McCurdy could do it — and I can't. It sounds well and looks plausible, boys, but in sober fact the thing would be impossible unless we turned out every man on the islands and scattered 'em. And that's something I won't have on my conscience."

An uneasy murmur approved these words.

"But listen here, boys — I don't want to be king," went on Jim earnestly. "It's hard to explain, because I worked you up to it in the first place myself. Since then I've gone through a good deal and learned a lot of things. Times have changed, boys, and in a few years from now no man would be able to hold kingship here. But for myself, it's something I don't want." He paused, then smiled suddenly. "Suppose you make Antoine king —"

"No!" roared the giant quickly. "I got de camp, de house, de fam'ly —"

"Well, why not Henri Gilbault?" urged Jim. The slight mutter of assent was pierced by the gaunt woodsman's shrill voice:

"Don' be de dam fool, Jim! What yon mean, eh?"

"It's hard to say just what I mean," returned Jim slowly, for now they were all intent upon him. "I've put it into a chanson, but it's hard to express in other words, boys. I don't want to be king. I want to come back into the woods and live *my* own life. Every man has his place, and my place isn't here but back at home — with yon. Now, there's one man down among you who can't refuse the kingship, and I give it to him with all my heart; but first, let me read you this chanson. It'll explain exactly what I mean, and although you may not understand it clearly —"

"Read it, Jim," broke in Antoine, "Mebbe we understan' pretty good, anyhow."

A low growl of assent urged on the words. Jim saw that their rage and bewilderment had passed into a slow doubt both of themselves and him, and the moment was opportune to present his own deeper feelings to them. He held up his paper to the dawn light, and read slowly and gravely, every word striking home to the men around him:

When God's hand touches mine in sure appeal,
To call me forth among the greater things,
I would it came where slow waves fade and steal,
And cedars fill the night with whisperings.

I crave no marble pile or carven name,
No rich memorial of high emprise;
In kindly memory my only fame.
My epitaph the warm love in men's eyes.

It is not mine to dream afar and seek
The Grails of pomp and power where others throng;
Let it be mine to know how Might is weak,
How Truth and Justice fare not with the strong!

Not mine to find the crown that greatness brings,
The hymn of triumph and the flame of swords;
Still let my hand shrink from the deeper strings
To touch the beauty of the minor chords.

No gift be mine of prophet's high insight,
No fiery eloquence of faith assailed;
Mine not to lead, but follow, after Right —
And if they will, let men deem I have failed.

Say this of me: He found peace after strife,
And trust in Nature's wisdom held him true;
His steps were cast in humbler walks of life —
Perchance God loved him, for his deeds were few!

The clear voice ceased. Deeply stirred by the utterance of his own thought, Jim looked at the men below him, but met no answering gaze. Big Antoine was leaning on his ax, staring hard at the wharf; little, rat-faced St. Peter was looking up at the sky, wide-eyed and rapt; Jean Tache seemed intent on the back of Gilbault's scrawny neck. From the crowded men behind, uneasy half glances flitted to Jim's face and away — until suddenly he flung out his arms in a great laugh of happiness, and all eyes went to him. He realized that in truth they had understood.

"Boys," he cried, vibrant with the joyous exultation thrilling him, "take Père Valerius for king — establish him here m his own spiritual kingdom! There's the answer to all of you — there's the king for you! Up to the mission, everyone, and pray for the men who died last night; then we'll go back into the peace of the woods and leave the new kingdom to its last and greatest king!"

The priest, startled, cried out. His words were engulfed in one great roar as Jim's speech caught the men's imaginations and fired them with splendor. Before Père Valerius could move, big Antoine caught him up; others rushed forward and lifted him to their shoulders, and with the roar of voices and stamp of feet resounding over the quiet harbor, the woodsmen filed away up the long wharf.

Jim leaped down to the quiet little figure waiting for him. He took Mary's hands in his, looked down into her eyes, and his arms went around her. Then, as his lips brushed her hair, she lifted her eyes to the dawn-filled east, and a low cry broke from her:

"Oh, Jim — the sky is so beautiful!"

www.ingramcontent.com/pod-product-compliance
Lightning Source LLC
Chambersburg PA
CBHW020141180626
46810CB00004B/1671